About the Author

Kerri has a passion for writing and all things fantasy, she absolutely loves what she does. She is a mum of five beautiful children; they are her inspiration in life. One thing she should say about herself, is that she is dyslexic and she fully believes, if you have a dream anything is possible. She loves to read and decided dyslexia was not going to stop her writing, so here she is now doing what she loves.

Becoming

K. Cooper

Becoming

Olympia Publishers
London

www.olympiapublishers.com
OLYMPIA PAPERBACK EDITION

A CIP catalogue record for this title is
available from the British Library.

ISBN: 978-1-80074-879-8

This is a work of fiction.
Names, characters, places and incidents originate from the writer's
imagination. Any resemblance to actual persons, living or dead, is
purely coincidental.

First Published in 2023

Olympia Publishers
Tallis House
2 Tallis Street
London
EC4Y 0AB

Printed in Great Britain

Dedication

I dedicate this book to my nan and grandad, my first fans and my biggest believers. Love you always!

Acknowledgements

Thank you to my husband and my parents for always believing in me, also my beautiful children for giving me inspiration.

For my husband, Danny, my mum, Geraldine, Dad, Paul and Nan, Dian. Thank you for always encouraging me to do what I love.

Also, for every dyslexic person who ever had a dream to write, don't ever let anyone say you can't... you can... I did!

Prologue

"What are you doing here? You can't be here; it's too dangerous," he whispered.

"You're her father! Where else am I supposed to go?"

He grabbed her by the elbow, leading her away. "Ellen, you must leave," he paused and let out a sigh, "Before anyone sees us together." Shame laced his voice as he stared her down.

"How dare you, she's your daughter! Yet you would still turn us away like we're nothing?" Pure shock shook her body, he was really going to do this.

"Don't make this any harder than it needs to be, please just leave before it is too late. I will provide you with whatever you need, as long as you leave now." His patience was wearing thin.

"Don't bother; we don't need your charity." Ellen turned her back and walked into the night. Clutching her three-day-old baby girl to her chest, she ducked her head and walked into the wind, never looking back.

"What can I do now?" She panicked. "I can't go home, not with a baby, not with his baby!" she told herself.

The wind whipped her hair into her face as she trudged on through the trees. She almost slipped a few times but managed to catch herself at the last moment. Rain poured down between the branches, soaking her from head to toe. Tucking her precious bundle closer to her chest, she pushed forward, not knowing which direction to go in. Only knowing she would not go back towards him or her family; she would raise this child alone.

The last nine months had been so hard for her; she had to conceal her growing belly from her all-knowing family, at the same time as carrying on as normal. The task was not easy. She kept to herself mostly, opting for all the solo chores, jobs or errands that needed doing.

Once the time arrived to have her baby, she had to seek out help from people she barely knew. Her family was not to find out about her pregnancy; it was the last thing she wanted for the tiny life growing inside her. She didn't want her child to grow up the way she had. It was not a life she wished upon anyone.

Alone and scared, Ellen had stumbled into the forest and practically dragged herself to the hut hidden well within its depths.

Banging on the door took everything she had, before the next horrific contraction gripped her body like an unyielding vice. An old woman cracked the door open and stared down at her.

"Ah, I wondered when I would be seeing you," she croaked with a smile. "Girls, help her in, and get ready. A babe is on its way."

Chapter 1

"Dear diary, today is my seventeenth birthday... yay me, Thea Jameson is finally allowed some independence... I hope." Thea read what she had just written in a sarcastic tone. "Yeah, right, like my mother would ever truly allow that," she scoffed.

"Thea, come down; I have a surprise for you," her mother shouted up to her.

"Coming," she answered. There was no point delaying, her mother would only keep shouting every couple of minutes, and she would never hear the end of it.

Flinging her legs off the side of the bed, she felt around until her foot found one of her pink teddy bear slippers. She jammed it in and searched for the next one. Shuffling along the carpet, she reached for the door and pulled it open,

"Here goes nothing then. Time to plaster the happy it's my birthday smile on my face once again."

Thea hated her birthday; it never turned out how it was supposed to. Her mum tried so hard every year to give her the best day, and she truly appreciated it. But it never changed the fact that she wasn't ever in the same place long enough to make any friends, to actually have a party or go out and celebrate. In fact, Thea just wished she could treat the twelfth of November as any other day, but no, her mother would never let that happen.

"There she is, my birthday girl," her mum said while giving her a hug, the kind that squeezes the air from your lungs. "Happy birthday, sweetheart." She handed Thea a little white package and a card. Her mum returned to the other side of the table and busied herself with whatever it was she was doing.

"Thanks, mum," Thea mumbled.

With a sigh, she unwrapped her gift. Inside was the most beautiful necklace she had ever seen; gasping, she looked up at her mum.

"It's beautiful, thank you," and for a change, she wore a true smile.

The pendant shone in the morning light, the palest blue and amber caught the rays in such a way, it looked as if tiny diamonds resided inside.

"You're welcome, darling," her mum didn't look up.

"Where did you get it? I have never seen anything quite like it before," she asked while fiddling with the chain.

The gorgeous gem was held snuggly in a silver casing, it looked like claws were grasping onto the precious jewel. Her mum hadn't answered,

"Odd," she thought. "Mum, you okay?" she questioned.

"Huh, yeah, I'm fine, love, sorry, what did you say?" her mum finally looked up. She looked sad somehow and lost in deep thoughts.

"Oh, I asked where you got my necklace from. I love it."

Thea's mum looked at her, she hesitated, and she was sure her mum's hands shook a little.

"Well, it's a long story really; it used to be your grandmother's, a long time ago," her mum stumbled over the words as she tucked her hair behind her ears.

She seemed nervous to talk about it, but Thea needed to know.

She had always been told that she had no other family, that it was just her and her mother.

"My Grandmother's, how? You said that there was nothing of our family left to show me?" she questioned.

"I know, I know, it's just I wanted to keep this one little bit as a nice seventeenth birthday surprise for you." Her mum forced a fake smile, and Thea knew it.

"Promise me, Thea, you won't ever take it off, not for anything or anyone," her mum urged.

"Of course, but why is it so important? What if I want to go in the shower! Can I take it off then?" she tried to joke.

"No, not even then," her mum snapped, cutting her off, but regained her fake smile quickly. "I just don't want you to lose it, darling; I'd be so sad if you did." With that, she kissed Thea on the cheek, "I have to go now, sweetheart, have a great day at school. I'll see you tonight for our special birthday dinner, okay?"

"Okay, but Mum, you know I'm in the sixth form now, right? I don't know if you can really call that school any more?" Thea called as her mum shut the front door. "That woman gets stranger by the day," she shook her head.

The walk to school – as her mum would put it – was the same as always. Same boring houses; followed by the same playing field and bus stop. It never took long to get there from their house, which was a good thing in a way. The only problem was; Thea felt even more alone once she arrived.

This would be school number eleven for Thea; she could never understand why they had to move about so much; her mum was always so vague about it. She had given Thea so many different reasons that she just stopped asking in the end. She had decided her mum was just a really restless person and couldn't sit still for more than a few months.

Secretly she hoped her mum was some kind of secret agent or something, but she knew her too well, and that could never be true. She liked baking cookies and sewing too much to be a secret agent.

There it was, Brockmoor sixth form, "Oh yay, here we go again," she muttered.

"Happy birthday, Thea," a voice called over the rush of people and noise.

That could only be one person, Jason. Thea had made at least one friend here. One person who didn't find her completely weird, not just because she was the new girl but the way she dressed and acted too. Thea liked to see herself as unique or individual. She had long mousy brown hair, it was never quite straight or curly, but that awkward in-between frizz she hated so much. Paired with her short, averagely built frame, she felt she was just plain and a bit dull to look at. There was one thing she liked about herself, though, and that was her eyes. They never seemed to stay one colour for long. She loved how she never quite knew if they were blue or green one day, or even hazel and grey the next.

Today she had attempted to tie her hair back in such a way that it looked as if she had some amount of control over it, which in truth, she didn't, but at least she had tried.

"Hey Jason, how are you? And please, no birthday talk; the less people know, the better," she muttered to him while punching him on the arm

"Ouch! Come on, Thea, you only turn seventeen once; let's celebrate," he chuckled, knowing all too well another punch to the arm was coming his way.

"Oh, look it's weirdo's birthday too," came a stuck-up voice from across the hall. Thea rolled her eyes.

"Oh, great, Miss Princess now knows it's my birthday too," she huffed.

Valarie was the most popular girl in Brockmoor sixth, or so she liked to think. When really, she was nothing more than a very rich, heavily made-up bully; that no one wanted to cross.

"It's Valarie's birthday today too, Thea," Jason whispered in her ear.

"Great, just great," Thea knew she was in for some fun now.

"So, you think you can have the same birthday as me, do you weirdo?" Valarie wore such a smug look on her face. She always did when she thought she was being clever and funny.

Thea had to stop herself from laughing. "Uh, Valarie, you are aware we don't get to pick our birthdays, right? We are born on those days," she said back

"Well, yes, of course I know that. Are you trying to say I'm stupid?" Valarie shot back as her face grew redder, and people sniggered behind their books.

"Me? Say anything like that about you?" Thea said in mock astonishment.

"Well then, good, keep it that way," Valarie flicked her long, straight blond hair over her shoulder and started to sway her hips as she walked away. "Oh, and weirdo, don't do anything to ruin MY special day, or you will be sorry."

They waited a whole thirty seconds before bursting with laughter.

"Who does she think she is, honestly," Thea struggled to catch her breath.

"She's something else," Jason agreed. She linked her arm in his.

"Come on, weirdo number two, we best get to class."

Her day wasn't as bad as she thought it would be. Valarie made a few more of her dumb comments like she always did. Today, her favourite insult was to call Thea a tree-hugging hippy wannabe, which made no sense, but she was thrilled with herself for coming up with it.

The name-calling would really irritate Jason more than it would Thea. He had been so sweet to her from her very first day. He was a quiet sort of guy; with short copper hair that kind of stuck up at odd angles regardless of what he tried doing to it, making him appear even taller than he already was. He wore black-rimmed glasses, and he always had his superhero rucksack slung over one shoulder. Thea found him sweet, in a brother kind of way. She loved him, though, for being with her every single day through the hellhole that is Brockmoor Sixth.

"What you doing later, weirdo number one?" he asked her with a nudge.

"Oh, I'm having a birthday dinner with my mum, it's this thing we do every year… stupid, I know, but it's tradition." Thea felt a bit nervous admitting her little dinner tradition to Jason.

"No, it's not stupid at all. I do the same with my gran each year on her birthday too. She loves a good birthday meal, or is it the sherry she loves more? I never know the difference," he laughed out loud.

A lot of the time, Jason's jokes were only funny to Jason himself.

"Anyway, if you're finished early or maybe even the weekend if you prefer, I thought, well, maybe we could go and celebrate," he paused. "You know, by like going to see a film or going bowling or anything really," his cheeks flushed.

He was struggling to get across what he meant; Thea had an idea that he might like her, but the blushing confirmed it.

She was flattered, of course; she just didn't see him that way.

"Sure, that would be great, I haven't ever had a birthday celebration with a friend before, just my mum, so I look forward to it. I'll text you once I'm done, okay," she called over her shoulder as she walked past the last few houses to her front door.

"Mum, I'm home," Thea called from the porch, but no answer came. "Mum! You home?" she called again, a bit louder this time. Still no answer.

Walking into the living room, she found it was empty; just her mum's favourite coffee mug sat on the table. She felt it, but it was stone cold.

"That's weird. She's normally home before me," Thea made her way into the kitchen. There, upon the kitchen counter, was a note next to the shopping bags that had not been unpacked yet.

The note read:

"Thea, darling, sorry I'm not home, but you need to leave now and go to this address. It is safer there, I promise. I'll explain everything later once I know you are safe. I love you, sweetheart. Go quickly."

At the bottom was a hastily scrawled address that she could barely make out.

Thea was totally confused. She did the first thing that came to mind. She rang Jason. "Hey, that was quick; you okay?" he sounded worried.

"Something is wrong! I need your help. Can you get here soon as you can?" she let out the breath she had been holding,

"Of course, I'll be right there," he didn't even hesitate. No more than five minutes had passed when Thea heard Jason running up her driveway. He didn't even wait for her to open the door; he just barged right on in. "Thea, what's wrong? Where are you?" he sounded so panicked.

"Kitchen," she called back. She hadn't even put the note down yet; she just kept staring at it. "Something is wrong, my mum left me this strange note, she sounded scared," she passed him the note. "I don't even know where that address is, how am I meant to get there if I don't know the way?"

She felt sick to her stomach. What if something really was wrong with her mum? What would she do?

"Oh, that's okay, I know where this is, and I can show you if you like." Jason just grinned at her; he liked the idea of swooping in to Thea's rescue.

"Great, let's go." Thea was already grabbing her coat.

"What now? It's like an hour's walk away," he complained

"Jason, did you even bother to read the note; clearly it's important that I get there ASAP, so are you going to help me or not," she said impatiently.

"Yeah, sure, of course I am, don't worry, sugar, I'll get you there," he smiled at her with that crooked little grin she liked.

"Did you really just call me sugar?" She laughed as his face turned red. "Oh come on, Mr smooth talker, we got us some walking to do." She grabbed him by the sleeve and pulled him out the door.

It didn't take them long to get to the address Thea's mum had written. It was only a few streets away.

"I thought you said it would take an hour to get here," she teased him. He just smiled at her.

Thea had never been to this part of town before. "Jason, what is this place? It looks so deserted," she looked around. There was an eerie feeling settling in her stomach."

"Umm, I think it used to be the street where all the old factory workers lived, or so my gran once told me," he replied.

The whole place looked black and grey; there were no lights or colour anywhere. It felt incredibly cold around this part of town. No one else seemed to be walking around here either.

"It's like a ghost town," she whispered. "What happened

here? The whole place looked as if it was covered in smudges of black soot, like it had been burnt. "Are you sure we are in the right place, Jason?" Thea was starting to doubt his sense of direction?

"I'm sure, this is Michael's Street, see it says so on that sign, well, half a sign, but it still says it." Jason tried to crack her a smile and lighten her mood; she seemed so tense.

Up ahead, a big imposing building loomed out of the gloomy sky above them. It felt as if it could bend down and crush them.

"This is the factory, I take it," she said to Jason with her hands on her hips and looking up at it. "What kind of factory was it exactly?" she asked

"I think it was a glove factory or something like that." Jason wasn't really paying much attention; he was too busy staring at the empty smashed-up windows to hear what she was saying.

"Wait, did you see that?" Thea had stopped dead in her tracks.

"See what?" Jason was turning in circles now, looking for something, anything really. This place was starting to give him the creeps, but he refused to look like a coward in front of Thea.

"I was sure I saw something move up there in that window. She pointed up and to the left. The wind picked up just at that point, making both of them jump; the noise was like a high-pitched scream.

"Want to hold my hand, Princess?" Jason teased, trying to hide that it had scared him just as much.

"Oh, shut up, hero, you jumped higher than me." They both laughed with racing hearts. "But seriously, did you see that person up there? I'm sure it was a person." Thea knew she hadn't been seeing things.

"It was probably just a cat, Thea, come on, let's find the

house you're looking for and get this over with," he urged her on. "It's just cold, and I'd rather be doing something else, to be honest, I didn't think anyone lived in this part of town anymore," he was puzzled, he had always been warned away from here as a child. "What number was it again?" he asked her.

"Seventy-three," she called out. "Wait; don't leave me behind." She ran to catch him up; she hadn't realised he had gone so far.

"Over here," Jason pointed to a door. The house looked just as bad as all the rest. There was row after row of terraced houses, all with some form of burn mark or soot-covered walls; and half were missing roof tiles.

"Surly, this is wrong." Thea began to say when she saw the door creak open. Thea edged closer to Jason; she even linked her arm with his and almost clutched his hand. "Why is this bothering me so much?" she wondered.

"Are you Thea Jameson?" an old man poked his head out of the door.

"Yeah, that's me. Is my mother with you?" She took a step forward. "She left me a note saying to come here?"

The man just stepped aside and opened the door wider. Clearly, she wasn't going to get any more information from him.

She walked towards the door with Jason still linked to her arm. She had no intention of walking in there alone.

"The boy cannot come in, Miss Jameson, only you." She stopped to stare at him, then at Jason in turn.

"Sorry mate, she's not going in there alone. We don't know who you are or what is going on, so no, she will not go without me," Jason felt absolutely nothing like he sounded. He was not brave in the slightest, in fact, he was terrified, but he wasn't allowing Thea to go in there on her own.

Thea felt oddly proud of him right then. He was being a true friend and a proper gentleman; she couldn't help but smile.

The old man huffed. "Fine, it's on your heads, though," he mumbled as he let the pair pass.

Chapter 2

Inside, the house wasn't much better than outside. It was so dark; only a few gas lanterns sparsely spaced along the long corridor flickered against the walls. Books covered the floor and were scattered in small piles as far as the eye could see. Thick dark velvety drapes hung over all the windows, denying any light entry into the gloomy chambers. Cobwebs hung in every corner, and there was a musty smell filling their noses with every breath.

Thea grabbed Jason's hand. All worry of coming across as anything but nervous and a bit scared was out the window as soon as the door had closed behind them.

"Where do we go? This is so creepy. Why would my mum send me here?" Thea's voice shook a little.

Jason squeezed her hand.

"I don't know, but don't worry, I won't leave you," he reassured her.

"Enter," boomed a demanding voice.

Thea looked at Jason. "It's now or never, I guess."

The old man had reappeared and was ushering them through a doorway, previously covered by a long thick black curtain. Gripping Jason's hand, Thea stepped past the man and into a candlelit room.

Seated in five high back, ornate-looking chairs were two men and three women; dressed in what Thea could only imagine were robes and cloaks.

The centre-most chair was occupied by an older woman with

sandy coloured hair, piercing green eyes, and a glare that was meant to intimidate.

Immediately to her right was a gentleman that looked to be around sixty years of age. He wore thin metal-rimmed glasses which sat proudly upon his face. He stared Thea square in the eye, yet she was sure she could see a slight smile tugging at the corners of his mouth.

On the left was another of the three women. She was a lot smaller than the rest, but by no means less imposing.

Finally, on either end of the table sat two younger-looking people, probably in their early thirties. One was a tall, dark-haired man; he had striking blue eyes and dark glasses and was wearing black robes. On the opposite end was a woman with long dark hair tied at the back of her neck. She had dark hazel eyes and olive skin.

Thea committed their faces to memory. She had many talents; ever since she had been small, she could never seem to forget a face.

"Thea Jameson, step forward, please," a raspy old voice called across the table.

She took a step into the room, closely followed by Jason.

"Who is this with you? Did we not state to come alone?" the same voice hissed at her.

"Uh, actually, no, you didn't. I had one simple note left for me by my mother saying to come here; and that it was safe," Thea blurted out. "In fact, where is my mother, she is meant to be here, and frankly, no, I don't think this place feels safe at all." Thea took a breath. "And this is Jason; he won't be going anywhere," with that, Thea clutched hold of Jason's hand and yanked him closer to her side, proving her point.

She held the gaze of the old woman who had spoken before;

she was not going to be pushed around by these people, whoever they were.

"Very well, young lady; but you would be wise to remember to hold that tone with your elders; I'll let your ignorance go this time, but do not make the same mistake with me again."

This woman was going to be a challenge, Thea thought.

"My name is Margret, high councilwoman of the Brockmoor witches." She paused for effect, but Thea had no idea what she was talking about; her face clearly showed it, too.

Sighing, the old woman continued, "To my right is Grace; the newly elected leader of our coven." Grace nodded to Thea. "On my left is Simon, he is also a high councilman to our coven as well as many other things," she smiled in his direction. He just nodded in response. "And finally, this is Jolene and Daniel, our newest council members," she pointed to her far left and right. Thea nodded to both but got nothing in return.

"Nice to meet you all, but what am I doing here? You all seem to know me, yet I don't know any of you?" Thea questioned.

Heads turned towards each other in confusion.

"What on earth are you talking about, girl? Of course you know who we are? Your mother would have told you everything you needed to know about your lineage as you grew up, so do not play coy with me." Margret accused, yet Thea still looked lost.

"My lineage? What are you on about? It's only my mum and me." The room felt as if it had grown colder all of a sudden, and Thea shuddered.

"She's telling the truth," came a voice from the other end of the room. It was Jolene; she had moved so silently from her chair. "She really doesn't know who we are." She hid a smile; something amused her.

28

"Look, people, not that I'm not grateful for the awkward welcome and the cold atmosphere, but seriously, where is my mother and what is going on?" she looked at each face in turn. "And that's another thing, really, come on, you can't be serious, right, witches; with wands and broomsticks and those silly pointed hats," she snorted in mock laughter. What kind of fool do you take me for?"

"Thea, I don't think they're joking; they look pretty serious to me," Jason urged her. Thea felt numb.

"I want to see my mum! Right now!" She'd had enough and was not prepared to deal with these strangers any longer.

She felt as if there was a storm brewing behind her eyes. Heat rose to her cheeks; she was so angry, so fed up with being left in the dark.

"Fine, fetch Ellen, from the looks of her, she has no control over her emotions, and frankly, I do not want to be cleaning that mess up when she cracks," Margret said, rolling her eyes.

"Thea, darling, it's okay. I'm right here, and there is nothing to worry about." Ellen rushed over to her daughter. She looked a bit concerned when she spied Jason but said nothing of it.

"What is all this, Mum? What is this place, and why do they all seem to know me?" Questions tumbled from her mouth, all directed straight at her mother.

"I'll explain it all, sweetheart, but right now, you really need to do whatever the high council asks, okay?" her voice trembled slightly; never had Thea seen her mum look so nervous.

"Wait! What, you're saying this is all real? How can it be real?" the look from her mother soon stopped her mid-question. "Fine, what do I have to do?" she breathed heavily.

"It's simple, child. Just show us your powers," Margret said with a smug smile.

"High councilwoman, she can't. She has been spelled so that her magic is suppressed for her own protection." Ellen sprang to Thea's rescue.

"Nonsense woman, she is seventeen now. All such things would have been lifted on her seventeenth birthday; surely you know this?" Margret was growing impatient.

"Please don't make her; I have spent her whole life protecting her. If she touches her power now, they will know where she is. They will come for her," Ellen begged.

"I'm sorry, my dear, but we need to know." She actually looked as if she truly did care.

"Come for me? Who will come for me?" Thea panicked,

"Don't worry about that now, love. Just do as they say so this can be over with," her mum reassured her.

Worry and regret marred her mother's beautiful face.

"I don't know how, though? What do I need to do?" She felt as if she were about to cry; this was all too much.

"Calm down, dear, just relax and let yourself feel the magic flow through you. If it's there you will know." Margret was trying for a soothing tone, but she achieved impatient instead.

Thea breathed out and felt herself go steady. She closed her eyes and waited; nothing happened. She peeked out from underneath one eyelid, only to see all eyes turned on her. She slammed her eye shut.

"Please, please, please just get this done, so I can go home." She clenched her fists so hard; she was sure she could feel a slight tingling in her hands, it could be her imagination, but she went with it anyway.

"Something is happening; I can feel it," she murmured. All of a sudden, she was roasting hot, like she was on fire. She wanted to scream but couldn't find her voice or grab anything to make the burning stop, but she couldn't move.

"Stop her now, it's too much. They already know she's here; her power is too strong, too uncontrolled." Daniel had jumped to his feet. He was shouting at everyone else in the room. It was the first time he had actually shown any interest throughout the whole meeting.

"She doesn't know how Dan; you're going to have to help her," Jolene's voice broke through the heat and pain.

With that, two strong hands clasped around both sides of her face, and immense pressure built up behind her eyes; so strong she thought she was going to die for sure, then nothing, this blissful blackness came over her. The last thing Thea knew was she was falling where the welcoming floor awaited her.

Hours had passed by the time Thea had woken up; she was laid in a large bed that was definitely not hers. It was covered in silken bed sheets and velvet throws.

"Mum," she shouted.

"I'm here, darling, don't worry, you're safe now," her mum's hand appeared on her forehead. "You're still a little hot mind; maybe you should stay in bed for a while longer," she urged.

"No," she pushed her way up until she was sitting. "You have a lot of explaining to do, and don't fob me off with excuses this time. I'm not as stupid as you might think," she glared at her mother. "Where's Jason, don't say you left him in there with those crazy people." She panicked and tried to force her way out of bed.

"I took him home, well, one of the others did, don't worry, his memory has been wiped so he won't remember any of this," she reassured her.

"Oh, great mum, sounds brilliant. You wiped my only friend's memory of the crazy you have dragged us into. Just brilliant, thank you so much. HAPPY BIRTHDAY TO ME, HUH?" Thea practically screamed in her mother's face. She was furious; and fed up with being kept in the dark. She was being treated like a child. Well, that ended today, she had a right to know what was happening in her life, and she intended to find out right now.

"I deserved that; I know," her mother sounded defeated when she admitted it.

"Start talking, mum, why am I here and who am I hiding from? As I just don't have a clue, I know nothing," she said. "Everything I thought to be real, seems to have been a lie; now nothing I knew was true." Thea felt lost and full of a heavy sorrow she couldn't explain.

"Look, Thea; darling, I never meant to hurt you. I was trying to protect you for as long as I could."

Thea cut her mum off mid-speech. "Protect me from what? What could possibly be after someone like me? I'm nothing, just boring old Thea Jameson."

"That is where you are wrong. We are part of one of the highest; most powerful witch covens the world has ever known, and when I had you, I knew I had to leave as if I didn't, they would have taken you away from me and used you for their own selfish gain." Ellen looked at the ground when she spoke, she didn't know how to face her daughter. "I hid my pregnancy from them, and when it was time for you to arrive, I ran away to the woods, to a small hut. An ancient outcast witch called Mary helped me," she continued. "My bloodline is very strong. I was taken from my parents at a very young age. I don't remember a lot about my family, but I was told my father was one of the most dangerous warlocks in history, and his power runs through my veins." She paused.

"I was to marry a man of the coven's choosing. They had picked him out for me already; they had my whole life planned out for me, but I fell in love with someone else, and that is where you come in." She finally looked at Thea. "If the coven were to find out about you, I would be severely punished, and I would never see you again. So, I ran, and I have hidden us ever since."

Ellen let out a very long sigh of relief, she had held all that in for seventeen years, and it felt wonderful to let it all out.

"Okay, so you're telling me I'm part of a secret society that has no clue until now that I existed, and they have been searching for you for seventeen years all because you have some super powerful blood?" Thea had her fingers pressed to her temples. "Great, that is just great, so what? Am I as strong as you then, and once they catch me, I'll be used for experiments and stuff?" she paused.

"No, darling, you are much more powerful than me. You proved that this evening and that was without ever using your magic before, you were incredible," she breathed. She was in awe of the daughter.

"How? I should only have a diluted amount of what you have, being your daughter, whereas he was your father, so you should be stronger?" she questioned.

"Ah, well, that's where it gets a bit messy. Your father is also a very powerful person, Thea. So powerful that it is forbidden for our kind to even converse with his kind." Ellen stared at her. "You, my dear are one of a kind; you will go down in history."

Thea spent the rest of the evening trying to make sense of what her mum had just told her, of how much she had to learn in a very small space of time, and what she was going to have to do now to stay safe.

Many of the Brockmoor coven members tried to visit her,

but she refused to see them, except Daniel and his sister Jolene. She wanted to thank him for stopping the pain and the heat earlier. She didn't know what would have happened if he hadn't been there.

Ellen was reluctant to leave when they entered, but Thea insisted she wanted to speak to them alone and that she would be fine for a while.

The room Thea was currently occupying was drab, dull and an old kind of feeling room. She had a beautiful four-poster bed though, which was in fact really comfortable. There were only a couple of gas lamps on either side of the room and a musty-looking rug in the centre of the floor. Other than that, the room was pretty dark and gloomy.

Ellen left, and her place was taken by Jolene; Daniel chose to stand at the end of the bed. He seemed so distant. Jolene, on the other hand, was the total opposite. She was bubbly and chatty. She seemed really nice and kind, someone she felt she could learn to trust, if trust was even the right word to use.

"How you feeling, Thea? That was quite an impressive show of raw talent you have going on there." Jolene was pretty impressed. "With a bit of help and training, you could certainly be formidable." Yet Daniel said nothing, just stared.

"Thanks, I think," was Thea's reply. "To be honest, I don't really know what's going on. How am I meant to handle this new world?" she continued. "Where do I even start to begin to understand any of this?" she asked.

"Well, first off, we need to work out the origin of your power, what element you are strongest at, and how much control you can master in a short time," Daniel finally spoke to her.

"I don't know who my father is if that is what you are asking," she replied; she felt a bit unnerved.

Her mum had just said everyone would want to know about her power and her family, so she decided it was best to stay quiet about the very small amount she knew.

"Yes, your mother hasn't said either," he replied. "I'll ask Margret if you could spend some time with Jolene for your training, frankly, she is the best teacher here; there is no point wasting time on any of the other bumbling idiots they have in this place," he turned to leave.

"Daniel, before you go, I just want to say thank you for your help today," she said.

"Don't worry, it's what I do," he replied and then shut the door behind him. Thea slumped back onto her pillows. She was exhausted.

Her hair had tumbled out of the bun she had attempted to put it in that morning and was flowing over her shoulder. She reached up and twiddled with the ends like she always did when she had a lot on her mind. "Well, he's a delight," she muttered.

Jolene laughed out loud. "Give it time; he does soften." Silence filled the room once more.

"Who is coming for me?" she asked Jolene without looking at her. "What do I have to do, and be honest, how much do I need to worry?" she had sat up and looked Jolene square in the eye.

"Look, Thea, the coven your mum is from is called The Willows. Any and all Willow witches are powerful; they rarely have births into the coven, they normally seek out powerful unclaimed witches or witches from weaker covens that they can overpower. Your mother is so lucky to still be alive, seeing what she did," Jolene explained. "You see, once a Willow witch, always a Willow witch, you are not allowed to leave, your mum ran away, and with something as special and rare as a child born to a Willow witch," she continued. "I'm not going to lie to you

Thea, but you have a hell of a ride in front of you. And that's only if whoever your birth father is, isn't interested in finding you too. If he is, well then. Who knows what will happen?" she finished.

"Wow, talk about being the bearer of bad news there, Jolene, thanks." She tried to sound as though she was joking, if only to hide how terrified she really was.

Jolene stood up. "I got to go, but I'll sort it so that we will start your training as soon as you are ready, okay? See you soon, Thea, and stay safe." Jolene waved as she shut the door.

Chapter 3

The next morning, Thea woke to the sun streaming in through her window. Her mum was busying herself, trying to make the room more homely. Thea watched her mother silently. She knew every inch of her by memory, but right now, she felt as though she didn't know her at all.

She had the same shoulder-length dark brown hair, the same caring light blue eyes. She was the same height as Thea and almost the same build. Yet Thea felt the woman standing in front of her was totally different somehow.

"Mum, what are you doing?" Thea asked

"Ah darling, you are awake. Well, seeing as we will be staying here for a while, I thought it would be nice if we tried to make the best of our situation." She smiled over at Thea.

"But Mum, my coursework, my friends… well, Jason anyway, and all our stuff at our house, we can't just leave it." She rambled on for a few minutes.

"Don't panic, I rang your school, and I told them you were really unwell. Jason doesn't remember anything, so he thinks you're unwell too, and our stuff is fine. Margret spelled the house so no one can enter unless it is us or we are there." She smiled once more and carried on dusting the room.

"Great, so I have no say in this? We have to just stay here as long as they choose?" Thea's mood was not improving.

"Right, up you get, and enough of this miserable mood. You always wanted to know about your family and where you came from, well today is the day." Ellen was so cheery this morning it was scaring her. Thea was practically dragged out of bed and ushered into a bathroom that hadn't seen any action for a fair few years.

"Uh, Mum, I need my clothes and wash stuff, you know... that are at our house... where we should be," Thea called back.

"There are new clothes in the cupboard, and all new wash stuff in the bathroom; just use whatever you like, love. I can easily make more." she answered

"What did she mean by 'make more'?" Thea thought, but she just shook her head and got on with it. Her life was really strange right now, so ignoring what her mum had said was much easier to handle.

A few minutes later, a clean, fresh feeling, Thea emerged from the bathroom. She had chosen a brand-new pair of high wasted black skinny jeans, which she coupled with a blue and black double layered lace top. She loved it the minute she set her eyes on it. She had brushed her hair back into a high ponytail and applied a little bit of eye makeup.

"You look lovely, Thea. I thought you might pick that top," her mum smiled at her.

"Thanks, mum. What do I do now then?" she asked with a shrug.

"Take the stairs all the way to the bottom and turn right, go down the corridor all the way to the end and on the left will be a brown old looking door, knock and wait, that is Margret's office, and Thea, please remember to knock and wait, don't go straight in." Her mum was very adamant.

"You're not coming with me?" She was nervous.

"I wish I could, darling, but this is just for you. If your mummy accompanied you everywhere, you would never learn anything," she hugged her daughter. "You will be fine. I just know it."

The walk to Margret's office wasn't as bad as Thea had thought. The house she was staying in was massive and much grander on the inside than on the outside. Considering the outside looked like a rundown, old, burnt-out wreck.

"It must be hidden or something," she thought as she walked down the seemingly never-ending grand staircase.

She ran her fingers along the banister. The fine, dark polished wood was smooth to the touch. She looked every which way she could. Old portraits hung on all the walls, from the very top to the very bottom. They became newer as they got lower down.

At the very bottom of the stairs, positioned in front of the main doorway, was a brand-new portrait. It was of the newly appointed head of the coven, Grace. Her long silky blond hair flowed over her shoulders, and her piercing green eyes stared straight ahead. The whole image portrayed importance. Thea stared at the painting for a while, wondering what it took to be where Grace was now; she didn't even really understand what she was doing here herself, let alone anyone else.

The floors of the lobby were gleaming; you could almost see your face reflected back. Large candle chandeliers hung from the high vaulted ceilings.

All the windows, bar two, were covered in the same thick dark velvet drapes she had seen the day before, yet there wasn't any of the cobwebs or dust that was present last time. There were certainly no piles of books scattered around; instead, they were neatly arranged on numerous bookcases dotted throughout the hallways.

Thea spotted the corridor her mum had told her to take. She

skipped down the last few steps of the stairs and practically skidded around the corner. It was odd to her that she hadn't come across anybody else since leaving her room; she was sure this place would be bustling, given how many people tried to visit her the night before.

Ahead of her was a long corridor with only a few doors scattered along its length. She did as her mum instructed and went to the last door on the left. She hesitated before knocking, she was so nervous, yet she didn't really know why.

"Enter," boomed Margret's voice. Thea jumped out of her skin; she had her hand raised, ready to knock, when the voice bellowed through the door. Slowly she turned the old round metal handle. There sitting in a high-backed, dark wooden chair, was the high councilwoman.

"Ah, Thea, at last, you are here. I was beginning to wonder if you were ever going to show," she said sternly. Thea smiled sheepishly.

"Hi, yes, sorry I'm late. I didn't realise there was a time limit," Thea caught herself before she said anything too rude.

"Come on, never mind, let's get started," the older woman hurried her along. "Basically, we need to teach you everything you should have learnt throughout your whole life before you are found," Margret said in a matter-of-fact voice. "And frankly, I don't know how long we have, no thanks to that explosion of magic you produced last night," she went on.

"Excuse me, ma'am, but you told me to show you, and seeing as I had absolutely no idea what you were talking about, I honestly think you should be taking the blame for that one, don't you?" Thea shot right back at her, there was no way she was going to have a bunch of people who claim to be high up in some coven, which she had no idea about; boss her around, then plant the blame on her for things she has no control over.

"Watch your tone, young lady; remember who you're talking to," Margret scolded.

"That's the thing, ma'am. I don't know you, I don't know any of you or anything about your world; so, forgive me for being lost, very confused and honestly scared," she admitted.

Margret stifled a comeback, she could see there was no point in pushing the matter. Thea was too fiery for that right now.

"Let's continue, shall we?" she said. "We here, in the Brockmoor coven, do more than just the everyday witch things you will find with other covens," she paused; Thea was still listening, which was good. "You see, we are one of the three original covens, so we have a lot more say in what goes on around here. Not only do we govern our own people, but we help to keep peace and control with other magical beings and races as well," she said with pride.

"Three original covens?" Thea questioned. "This wasn't going to be so boring after all," she thought.

"Yes, there is us; the Brockmoor coven, then the coven your mum came from, which is the Willow coven, and finally the Nightshade coven," she said with a sigh. "We barely speak of the Nightshade witches any more; nothing good comes of it."

Silence filled the room like a thick suffocating fog. Thea had to ask, though, "How come. Are they bad at what they do?" Margret just looked at her

"Oh, to be as ignorant as you, my child. They are a foul stain upon our kind, but right now is not the time or place to learn about the Nightshades. We have much more pressing matters to attend to. The history lesson will have to wait." Margret moved swiftly on. Thea left it; she knew when to not push her boundaries.

"Right, each day you will spend your morning with me, you

41

will learn all the laws and rules of our people. Come now, don't look so glum, it will be more exciting than you may think." Margret grinned at her, Thea was stunned; she hadn't seen a true smile from this woman, and now she had; she could see she was quite pretty, really.

"Then, after that, you will meet with Jolene, she will teach you all the defensive and protective spells, manoeuvre's and even the odd hex and curse you could possibly need, well, as much as she can in such a short time, and then finally, in the afternoon you will spend your time with Simon, he is going to teach you all about the magical world." Margret smiled again.

"Isn't that what you are teaching me?" Thea asked.

"Oh no, dear, I'm just teaching you law and rules. Simon will open you up to the whole magical world." Margret seemed to exist by the prospect of teaching Thea as if she was her own personal challenge.

"Okay then, when do I get my wand, broom and hat," Thea joked. Margret didn't find it funny at all.

By the time Thea was done with her morning lesson, she was exhausted, and she had only just begun. She still hadn't seen anyone else apart from Margret all morning. She left the office and wandered in the same direction she had come earlier. She thought she would spend the whole day trying to find Jolene, which she didn't really mind as this place was massive. She would love to get to explore it. No such luck; Jolene was waiting for her under a giant Grandfather clock Thea had missed that morning.

"Hey Jolene, I'm guessing you're here for me." Jolene smiled.

"I sure am," she touched Thea's shoulder. "Come on, I have loads to show you, but first I think you should get something to eat."

Thea stared at her in awe. "Are you a mind reader? How did you know I was starving?

Jolene laughed. "Well, actually, I can read your mind, yes, but it was your belly rumbling that gave you away," she had to laugh. "Come on; the kitchens are this way." She led Thea down a cold, stone corridor. It wasn't long before they arrived at a set of massive double doors.

The smells that were wafting out the doors were delicious, making Thea's belly rumble again. Pushing through the doors, they came face to face with a small rounded woman; Jolene said her name was Lucy, and she was the main cook here.

"Jolene, why are you always so late for lunch? Once again, I have packed everything away, and now I know I'll have to drag it all out again." The woman turned around to face them as she finished moaning at Jolene. Her whole face went red; she hadn't realised Thea was with her.

"Oh, I'm so sorry, I didn't know you had company," she stammered. "What can I do for you?" she finished

"Well," said Jolene. "Thea here hasn't eaten since, well, I don't know when, so if you could fix her up something Lucy, I would really applicate that," Jolene smiled sweetly.

"Of course, I won't be a moment." Thea felt sorry for the woman.

"So, what did you learn this morning with old Maggie," she asked.

Thea snorted. "Old Maggie, I'll have to remember to use that next time, and honestly, I can't remember; it was kind of information overload," she admitted.

"I know what you mean. Maggie taught Dan and me, it's her pace or no pace, I'm afraid." Thea just shrugged. A door opened across the room, a door Thea hadn't even noticed until then. A guy around her age, maybe a little older, walked in backwards, his arms were full of dirty dishes, and he had to try and shut the door and juggle his load at the same time.

He had dirty blond hair and he was quite tall from what Thea could see, but to be honest, she couldn't make out much from where she was standing.

"Who's that?" she asked Jolene and pointed at the boy. Jolene looked from Thea to the boy and back again.

"Who, that?" She pointed over her shoulder. "That's Ryder. He works here in the kitchen, as well as attending the occasional lecture with the other students," she answered.

"Oh, is he a witch too?" she asked

"Well, technically, everyone here is a witch, it just depends on the degree of magic you have and if you have mastered your element or not," she paused. "Young Ryder showed strong potential, but then it seemed to just fizzle out," she sighed sadly. "No one knows why; it's sad really, he's such a nice kid," she said. "He actually came to us from outside of our coven just like you, yet we still don't know where from. Problem is, the boy doesn't know himself, so makes it hard to place him you see," she finished. "Ah, here is our food, eat up you're going to need the energy."

Thea tried hard with Jolene; she really liked her. She was stern but fair with her teaching. She understood that up until yesterday afternoon, magic had not been real to Thea, that this was a whole new world to her. Even though Jolene kept Thea busy with defensive moves and protective stances, Thea just couldn't get her mind off Ryder, the boy from the kitchen.

She didn't get a good look at his face or at anything really, but he stuck in her mind like glue.

"Thea, remember I can read your mind. I'm not trying to; but right now, everything you think is projected to me as if you're screaming it in my face. I'll teach you how to shield your mind from others soon, but right now, that is too strong a spell for you to try."

Thea's face burned from embarrassment. She couldn't believe the things that were going through her head were heard by Jolene, too; she was mortified, and Jolene burst out laughing.

"Oh, come now, it's not that bad. He's cute and you're new, plus it's intriguing as he's like you in a way." Her attempt to soothe Thea's dignity was very sweet but failed miserably.

Thea had lost her focus now, and Jolene could tell; she felt kind of sorry for her, she shouldn't have embarrassed her like that, but it happens to everyone at some point. They might as well just get it out of the way now.

"Okay, let's call it a day, shall we? I think you have had quite enough training for one day, oh and Thea? Call me Jo." Jo winked at her. "Meet me by the clock same time tomorrow," she told Thea. "If you go and find Simon on the second floor, first corridor on the right and third door down on the left, you will find him in the library. He may want to start your lesson early." she waved Thea goodbye and left at quite a speed.

Thea slumped down on a low wooded bench with her sweaty head in her hands. She couldn't believe what had just happened.

"This is surreal. When will I wake up?" she asked herself. "Why me? I'm nothing special, I'm just me. I liked my old life, it was boring, but it was mine, and it was safe." She wasn't feeling like doing another lesson today, but she knew she had to, not because she didn't want to annoy Margret, but she didn't want to disappoint her mum.

"For goodness sake, come on, let's get this done." She

heaved herself up off the bench and dragged herself out the door in the direction Jo told her.

The library was breath-taking, never had she seen such a stunning room with so much natural light, filled from floor to ceiling with beautiful old wooded bookcases, all full to bursting with every kind of book you could imagine.

Simon was busy piling books high on one of the tables. It didn't look all that safe, really, but who was Thea to tell a man how to do his job? Simon spotted her before she had even fully entered the room, which was amazing, seeing how big the room was.

"Thea, over here, please." She walked towards the elderly man. He was dressed all in black today, with this greying hair sprawling all over the place. The last time Thea had seen him, he was immaculate. Not a hair out of place. Today it seemed he must have been too busy to concern himself with his appearance.

"I heard I would be seeing you today, so I have gotten your lesson ready now." He pointed at the table of books.

"Whoa, are you crazy? I can't read all those books today. That is massive amounts," she worried; what kind of girl do they think she is. She may have hidden magic she wasn't aware of, but she's not a superhero with amazing reading powers. Simon chuckled.

"These are not all for one day, trust me, I'm good, but I'm not that good. I couldn't teach you all of this in one day," he smiled. "I want you to come over here and pick the very first book up that grabs your interest. Don't even think about it; just pick up the first one that grabs you," he encouraged her.

"Umm, okay then." She looked at him a moment, then walked up to the table, placed her hand just above the books – she didn't even know why she did that, he hadn't told her to –

and moved them along until she felt a tingling in her fingers. It was dead centre on a book titled "*Songs of the Sea*." She picked it up and handed it to him. "I guess it will be this one then." He looked stunned and a tiny bit scared. "Okay, Sirens it is then." He exhaled and opened the book.

"Wait, what did you say?" She stopped him. "Did you say sirens? As in creepy mermaid-like people that lure sailors to their death? Because if so, that is crazy talk." Her eyes must have been bugging out of her head as Simon looked at her like she was talking a different language.

"Well, yes, of course I am. What else would I be talking about?" He genuinely looked confused.

"Okay then, my day has just officially gotten weirder."

Chapter 4

The moon was high in the sky by the time Thea got back to her room. Her mum was sat in the chair in the corner with a warm-looking blanket thrown over her knees.

"Hi honey, how was your day?" she asked her daughter as she shut the door.

"Long mum, it was long," she sighed. Thea was so tired, her body and mind had taken a beating today.

"I know it's a lot to take in right now, but something you learn here could save your life," Ellen said.

"I guess so, but if you had just told me when I was younger, I wouldn't be doing this now." Thea was in a foul mood tonight. She was struggling to come to terms with her new life, with everything she had to learn, and she still felt the sting of embarrassment from Jo hearing her thoughts.

"I know, and I'm sorry, but I had to protect you. I know it's a lot to ask, but I really hope you will forgive me," her mum said. "Do you want to talk about how your day went?" she asked her.

"No, Mum, I don't, I just want to go to sleep, and I have to do it all over again tomorrow, so if you don't mind, I'd really like to get to bed now." She didn't wait for her mum to reply; she dumped her stuff on the floor and started to pull back the covers on her bed. Ellen took the hint; she got up, kissed her daughter on the forehead and left quietly.

"Up, up, up, sleepy head." Thea's mum came bounding in full of cheer. She flung the curtains open and started to pull the blankets back. Thea wasn't there. She panicked; What if her old coven had found them? What if she had been taken and she never saw her daughter again.

The door to the bathroom opened, making Ellen jump.

"Oh, hey, Mum." Thea was drying her hair. She had gotten up early so that she could get a shower in before she had to go find Margret again.

"Thank goodness," her mum threw her arms around her neck. "I thought they had gotten you; I came in here, and you were gone," she practically sobbed.

Thea laughed. "Don't worry, I just needed a shower." She hugged her mother and then hurried out the door. "Sorry, I have to go," she called back to her.

Margret was waiting when she arrived. "Sorry I'm late, ma'am, my mum was an obstacle today." She pulled the chair out and sat down. "So, what are we learning today then, Maggie," she said with a grin. Margret was not impressed.

"Who told you to call me that?" she snapped. "Do not call me that again Thea. I don't appreciate it," she continued.

"Right, okay." Thea really didn't want to bother today; she hadn't gotten over the day before yet.

There was a knock at the door and Jo popped her head around the corner.

"Hi M, I wondered if I could have Thea first today? There is so much to teach her, and I really need to go help Dan with that errand, you know, the one from yesterday," she said, fully directing it at Margret as if she was pointing the blame for whatever it was Daniel was doing.

"Fine, take her now then, Jolene," Margret literally huffed.

"Great, come on, Thea. You're with me now," Jo grabbed

Thea by the arm.

"Oh, and Jolene, I would appreciate it if you didn't teach my students silly nicknames again, please," she pretended to scold her.

Everyone in the coven knew Jolene was Margret's favourite. Jolene just grinned.

"What's going on, Jo? Why are we rushing?" Thea was almost being dragged down the corridor by Jo.

"Nothing for you to worry about. I just need to make sure you know enough to get by with," she breathed over her shoulder.

"What is this about Daniel's errand?" Jo had stopped at her question.

"He has been tasked with a difficult job, one he shouldn't have to bear alone, so I have chosen to help my brother," she chose her words carefully. "I just have to prepare you first," she smiled.

Jo worked Thea so hard that morning. She actually mastered a protection spell and blocked a good amount of Jo's physical attacks. There weren't any signs of the pair slowing their pace or coming to a stop any time soon. That was until the door burst open, and Daniel charged in.

"Jolene, we got to go now," he yelled at her and turned and ran. Jo dropped everything and chased after him. She didn't even say goodbye to Thea.

Thea stood in the large practice hall alone, looking and feeling like a lost puppy. She was still stunned by Daniel's sudden entrance and how quickly the siblings had left. Her instructor just bailed on her, and she had no idea what was going on or what to do next.

The cute boy from the kitchen she had seen yesterday, walked into hall; he hadn't spotted her yet. He had headphones on and a mop in his hand. Thea stood there and watched him for a moment, until he looked up and finally saw her. He kind of half-smiled at her, then carried on mopping.

She took a step towards him, making him stop and look up at her again. He removed his headphones.

"Can I help you?" he asked her. She was a bit nervous but didn't know why.

"Uh, I'm Thea. I'm new here. Well, I arrived two days ago," she stammered out. "You're Ryder, right?" she asked him.

"Wow, I must get talked about a lot for the new girl to already know my name, but yeah, that's me," he seemed suspicious of her.

"Okay, cool. Jo said she thinks you and me are very alike." He stopped her by holding his hand up

"How are we anything alike? I'm a guy thrown out by his family for reasons I can't remember, whereas you're a girl who didn't even know she was a witch. To me, that says we are nothing alike." He suddenly seemed a little hostile.

"Okay then, sorry I said anything, news about me clearly travels fast too, and nice to meet you, by the way," she said petulantly and started to walk away.

"Look, wait. I'm sorry, that was unfair. I'm just tired of people asking me about my life. I feel like I'm being interrogated all the bloody time," he admitted.

"I get it, don't worry," she replied. He looked at her for a second. "Well, if you like, I could help you learn the basics; I heard you have to learn everything as soon as possible, that you could be in some kind of trouble," he offered, clearly trying to be nice and make up for his initial rudeness.

"Yeah, I guess so. The sad thing is I don't even really know why I'm in trouble or who I'm hiding from, I feel like I'm living in a bubble, and surely it should pop soon," she told him. He smiled at her; she really liked his smile.

Ryder propped his mob up against the wall and removed his headphones fully.

"Okay, first things first," he said. "Do you know your primary element?" he asked her. She met his question with a very confused look. "I'll take that as a no then," he laughed.

She couldn't fully concentrate. She kept looking at him, then noting things about him she hadn't seen earlier.

"Okay, next plan, I'll try the early basic primal test spells with you. We will soon see which you are strongest in," he ploughed on; oblivious to the scrutiny his features were being put through right now. "You have no idea what I'm on about, do you?" he asked

"Nope, but you look so serious, so I'll let you carry on," she laughed.

"Hey, don't mock me; I'm trying to help you here," but he was only playing; no malice came through in his voice. "What I'm going to do is call forth the elements to stand upon my hand, and then the one you can transfer to your own hand will be your primary element," he told her.

"Okay! But how do I do that? What spell do I say or whatever it is? I have never heard of this before. I have only been involved in magic for two days," she reminded him.

"You don't need to use a spell. If it's your element, it will come to you." Thea nodded understanding. "Ready?" he asked.

"Ready," she replied.

Ryder held out his hand and murmured a couple of words. Thea was sure the room filled with static electricity; the whole place was buzzing.

Ryder extended his hand out towards her; somehow, she

knew to copy him. Their fingers almost touching, she noted how much bigger his hand was than hers.

"Focus, right now is not the time to examine cute guy's hands," she silently scolded herself. Like lighting, all four elements jumped from Ryder's open palm to Thea's. Ryder's face was a picture of pure shock, then awe. Thea was confused.

"Umm, Ryder, didn't you say one primary element? Oh well, I'm sure loads of people have all four," she shrugged.

"No, Thea, they don't. In fact, it is incredibly rare for someone to have even two primary elements. I haven't ever heard of someone having all four," his voice shook as well as his hands. "I must get Margret, no grace, no both of them." He ran from the room without even looking Thea's way. She was just left there holding four tiny little elements in her hand.

"Huh, what do I do now then," she thought. The elements started to move around, which tickled. "Keep still, you guys. I don't want to drop you," she laughed

"We don't like being so close together," came a crackly voice. She was sure it was within her mind.

"Oh, wow, you can talk. Well, how about you move apart… as long as you don't hurt me, of course," she quickly added. She was filled with a warm feeling.

Before her eyes, she saw the tiny flame move up her arm and settle upon her left shoulder. The tiny water element slid its way along her chest and up to her right shoulder. She felt like she was wet wherever it had moved, but she wasn't, she was dry when she looked down. Finally, the tiny earth element jumped over to her right hand; when it appeared there, she felt as if she had caught a boulder, the weight quickly lifted, though, which left the tiny Wind element sitting snuggly in her left hand.

"Happy now?" she asked out loud to the elements. She

smiled when she was filled with every sensation you could imagine.

"Oh, my days, this is truly amazing, breath-taking, astounding." Grace's voice floated across the hall. "Never has this happened before, Thea, you are one very, very special girl," she said breathlessly.

Words exploded all around her; everyone started speaking all at once. News clearly travelled fast in this place. Thea's mum was pushing her way through the steadily growing crowd.

"Let me through. That is my daughter," she called as she pushed through the last few people. Her mum's face was just as shocked as everyone else's. "Darling, it's true, I didn't believe it, but now I can see it. I don't know what to say," she half spoke, half sobbed.

"I don't get what the big deal is, Mum. So what, I can hold all four elements in my hands; whoopee, lucky me," she said with a shrug, making the water and fire elements jump. "Sorry, guys," she said out loud. "They don't like it if I move too fast or if they are too close together," she told her mum

"How do you know that," her mum asked.

"Well, they told me, of course." Thea didn't realise hearing the elements was unheard of.

"Child, come here," Margret shouted. Thea rolled her eyes and moved towards old Maggie. "Did I hear you right? Did you just tell your mother that you can hear, understand and converse with the elements?" she asked

"Well yeah, sure I can, can't you?" she asked back.

"Of course I can't!" Margret spat back, only one other person in the whole of history could do that, and he's been dead a very long time." She turned her nose up at Thea.

"She is right. Only master James has been able to hear us.

54

It's been a very long time since we spoke to a mortal," the water element told her. She didn't know how she knew which one was speaking to her at which time – she just knew.

All afternoon Thea was questioned about her elemental abilities, and she could answer hardly any of the questions; she knew the least of everyone. She released her new tiny friends not long after the crowd had gathered. She had the feeling that the sheer amount of people was unsettling to them.

"What do you want me to say, Margret, that I fully know what is going on and that I can do whatever you ask me, because I can't." Thea was getting fed up with the same questions over and over. She was tired, frustrated and wanted to be left alone. "Are we done here? I'd like to go, and I need some space," she finally spat out. She couldn't stand one more minute of this constant interrogation. "Now I know how Ryder feels," she thought.

"You may go for now, but we will pick this up tomorrow," Margret made it very clear she wasn't done with her yet.

"Great, I can't wait," Thea said sarcastically. She was out of that door before anyone could even try to change her mind.

Walking along the corridor with her head down, she passed many people, all talking about her. She just wanted to get back to her room, away from the whispers and the stares.

Someone grabbed her by the wrist and pulled her around the corner. Her heart was in her throat; what would she do if it was someone bad, someone she couldn't fight off.

"I have been waiting all day to get to talk to you again," relief flooded her; it was Ryder.

"Ryder, you scared me," she breathed.

"Sorry, I didn't want anyone to see," he said. "Looks like you're a big deal around here now," he joked

"Oh yeah, great isn't it? I finally know how you feel with the constant interrogations; it's really horrible," she sympathised.

"What you going to do now then?" he asked.

"What do you mean? I have no idea what I was doing before. This changes nothing for me, it just means that I now have everyone watching me do it," she moaned. "All I want to do is go back to my own house," she confessed.

"I don't think that is a wise idea, Thea. It's probably crewing with people looking for you," he told her.

"Well, I wish I could at least go and get a few of my own things. I miss my stuff, all this new stuff is nice, sure, but it's not mine." She felt homesick and lonely. "Funny how this place was practically deserted yesterday, then all of a sudden it is crewing with people. Why is that?" she questioned.

"Well, they were all here yesterday, you just didn't see them as they were working, but as soon as word about you spread today, they all came running," he smiled sheepishly.

"Let me guess; you spread the word right?" she playfully poked him.

"Guilty, sorry." He faked a groan when she poked him.

Thea hadn't realised how very close the two of them were standing until then, and she finally got a really good look at the boy in front of her. Her heart rate picked up, and she was acutely aware of his breath on her cheek. She shifted uneasily. She panicked.

"What if he's a mind reader too?" she wondered.

"Hey, are you okay?" he asked her tilting his head slightly to see her better.

"Yeah, I'm fine. I better get going through," she edged out from between the wall and Ryder's body, trying desperately not to touch him; she knew if she did, she would feel the touch for

56

hours after.

"Oh, okay, no problem," he said as she slipped out from their hiding space. "Hey, how about we meet up tomorrow? Maybe we could think of a way to get a few of your things from your house," he asked her before she could turn the corner. Her head snapped around.

"That would be amazing. Yes, I'll meet you here tomorrow; I don't know what time, though," she said. "How will I know when to meet you?"

"I'll send you a message if you like," he suggested. "I don't have my phone, so that won't work," she started to say. He laughed quietly, his eyes shone though. Thea liked that.

"I have my ways," he nudged her playfully, her cheeks flushed.

"Okay, see you then." She did a little wave, which she instantly regretted, feeling stupid and made her way back to her room, where her mum would be waiting, of course.

Chapter 5

The end of the day couldn't come quick enough. Thea had been looking out for Ryder all day; he was nowhere to be seen. Granted, she had been hounded by everyone she passed about her elemental powers. Even the cook wanted to know something about her. She couldn't move without all eyes being on her.

Her lesson with Jo was so short she couldn't even call it a lesson; Jo was so distracted; she didn't really teach Thea anything she would really need to know.

Finally, five p.m. arrived and she was officially allowed to go and do her own thing.

Walking back to her room, she walked as slowly as she could. She didn't want to miss Ryder just in case he was someplace else, and not where they agreed to meet. She hadn't really allowed herself to get her hopes up about going to her house. She so desperately wanted to go home.

Wandering slowly back towards her room, she found her mind wandering to simpler times. She missed Jason and, oddly, the easiness of her old sixth form and classmates. In fact, she missed even having classmates. This learning on your own thing wasn't as fun as she thought it would be. She missed the noise of other people her own age; she missed being able to walk around outside and meaning nothing to every other person she passed.

Now that she knew she was a witch – a powerful, highly sought after one at that – made everyday tasks almost impossible.

The next thing she knew, she was being tugged to the left by her wrist. Her back slammed against the cold solid wall. Before she could shout at whoever grabbed her, a hand came over her mouth, followed by warm breath on her cheek and blond hair brushed the top of her head.

"Finally found you super star," came the voice she had been waiting to hear all day.

Ryder had found her at the only moment she hadn't been looking for him. Secretly she smiled to herself. "You scared the crap out of me, Ryder," she breathed. "And where was that message you were meant to have sent me?" she questioned.

"I know, but it was so worth it, and I'm sorry I lost track of time," he laughed.

"Says you," she pretended to be angry. "Where have you been all day?" she questioned him. "The last couple of days I have seen you around loads throughout the day, but today you were nowhere to be found?" she puzzled.

"Well, I had to set my plan in motion for tonight, didn't I?" he replied with a smug little smile,

"So, you have a plan, do you? And do you care to share?" she mocked. He still hadn't stepped back from her. She was still jammed up against the wall with his body inches away from hers.

"Well, there is this old tunnel that is very rarely used any more. It's not far from the kitchens," he explained. "The only problem is, it's not going to be easy to get to," he continued. "Seeing as you're now practically a celebrity around here, I'm going to have to try and find a way to hide you. They won't care about me coming and going as I please, not now you're around." He winked at her, but she could tell he was a little disappointed.

"Perhaps he liked the attention after all?" she thought. "Okay, so what do we do then? How will I get past?" she asked him.

He studied her, taking ages to reply. She started to get a little nervous under his gaze.

"Ryder, come on, what's the plan," she urged him.

"Sorry, yeah, well, my magic isn't as strong as yours, but I do have my own special little tricks," he said. "I can block my magic from others, meaning I can do magic and they won't be able to sense it or see it," he finished. "Pretty cool; huh?" he grinned.

"Pretty cool indeed," she breathed back. "I'm actually going home." she could hardly contain her excitement.

Fifteen minutes later, Thea and Ryder were standing just around the corner from the kitchens. Ryder had muttered some words right beside Thea's head just before stepping out from where they had been hiding. He reassured her that only he would be seen; he couldn't hide them both; it would just take too much energy from him.

Thea was scared; she had no idea what to do, she couldn't feel anything, and she didn't look any different.

"Calm down," Ryder mumbled to her. "I can hear you breathing, you're so loud," he laughed.

"Sorry, it's just scary," she answered in a harsh whisper. He ran his fingers down her arm.

"I'm right here, okay? I won't let anything happen," he lingered on her wrist before dropping his hand and walking around the corner. She had been so caught off guard by his way to intimate touch that she had to hurry to catch him up.

She tried to be as quiet as she could without getting left behind. The feeling of his fingers running down her skin was like electricity, and she loved it. Focusing ahead, she saw someone approaching, and she held her breath.

"Hey Ryder, you okay mate?" the newcomer said. He was

about Thea's age; give or take a year or two, shorter than Ryder with red hair.

"Hey Nathan, I'm good. You cool?" Ryder answered.

"I hear it was you who found out about that new girl's weird powers?" he remarked.

"Uh, yeah, it was me," Ryder said, hoping he didn't give anything away; he was pretty used to hiding magic, so he just hoped Thea could hide herself too.

"Always the way, isn't it? The people you least expect get all the cool things. I hear she doesn't even know how to do magic; shame really that such a talent is wasted on a nobody," he sniggered.

Ryder glared at him. "Nat, you don't know her, so don't make assumptions, okay?" his tone was harsher than he intended.

"Whoa, chill man, I didn't mean anything by it. Anyone would think you have a thing for her or something?" He shook his head. "She may have unbelievable talents that she doesn't even know how to use, let me remind you, but that doesn't mean she's any higher up in her abilities than your average six-year-old," he snapped. "God, you can get any girl here, don't waste your time on that one, is all I say." He turned around and left before Ryder could even reply.

Ryder didn't say anything until Nathan was well out of earshot, but Thea could see him shaking; she could feel his whole-body tremble in front of her. Lifting her hand, she placed it on his arm and waited until he turned his head.

"Thea, I'm so sorry you had to hear that. What a complete idiot," he quickly apologised.

"It's fine, don't worry, I have heard a hell of a lot worse," she replied. "Plus, it's true. I'm new to magic so I don't know a lot; he just sounds jealous, if I'm honest," she smiled at him.

She didn't say what she was really thinking, though. She wasn't sure if what Nathan had said was the truth or not, but if it was, then Ryder, the super-hot guy she just met, likes her, and this made her head dizzy.

"Come on, let's get going before anyone else comes, shall we?" he said as he moved forward.

There it was, the door that led to the outside. She wanted to yank it open and dash for freedom, not caring what dangers were waiting for her outside.

"Okay, stay close. It gets dark and narrow down here," he said over his shoulder. He didn't have to tell her twice, she inched closer until there were barely a few centimetres between them.

"Wow, it's cold down here," she whispered.

"Here, put this on." He handed something back to her. It was dark so she couldn't see what it was, but it was warm. She realised it was a jacket, his jacket. She pulled it on and snuggled into it; it smelt like him, and she felt like she was glowing.

"Won't you be cold?" she asked him, secretly hoping he wouldn't ask for it back.

"Na, I'm good with the cold, plus I want you to wear it," he answered.

They walked in silence for a few minutes, well, until Thea tripped over something and nearly fell flat on her face. Ryder had caught her.

"Careful now, I said it was narrow," he was so close to her again.

"Thanks," she breathed back.

He moved his hand to hers and laced his fingers with hers.

"Here, I'll make sure you stay on your feet," he chuckled. "Won't be long now, and we will be out," he finished saying.

Thea couldn't believe what was happening. She had only

just met this guy. She hardly knew a thing about him, yet she was so drawn to him. She was fully lost yet totally excited at the same time.

Flirting wasn't in her skill set. So, she decided to try and play it cool and just see what he did next.

The cool, fresh air was such a welcome treat; Thea hadn't ever thought she would miss it like she had.

Ryder held the old rusted door open for her.

"Can you imagine the drama that will be happening back there once they realise their new golden child is missing?" he laughed.

"Don't," she playfully punched him. "My mum is going to be freaking out," she said, only slightly worried.

"We better make this as quick as we can then," he said, still holding her hand. She had no intention of letting go first, and it seemed as if he didn't either.

"Lead the way, Miss," he said.

"I need to know where we are first." Ryder didn't know she was new in town.

"Oh, sorry, west side of town, near the new shopping centre," he told her

"Ah, okay, not too far from mine; I live quite close to the fire station," she told him.

"This way then." He led her off to the right. "My jacket suits you," he winked at her. She just smiled, hoping the sudden heat rising to her cheeks didn't show too much; he made her stomach do odd little flips when he looked at her that way.

The streets were much quieter than Thea thought they would be. But she wasn't complaining. She really liked Ryder's company, he seemed to be able to talk about everything and anything, and there never seemed to be any of those horrible awkward silences.

"Ryder, can other people see me now?" she asked him. "If they can't, then you must look so weird talking to yourself," she laughed

"Yeah, I dropped the spell once we stepped into the tunnel."

"Are you able to put it back on really fast if we need to, though?" she asked.

"Of course, don't worry," he reassured her. She stopped walking with a tug of his hand.

"What's wrong?" he looked worried

"Can you hide me now then, please? You see that group of girls coming down the road? They are from the sixth form I used to go to," she informed him.

"Sure," he smiled at her.

He muttered once again. This time Thea's ears popped a bit when the spell hit in. He still held her hand, which must have looked weird, until he pulled their joined hands behind his back. He stepped sideways to let the group pass.

One of the girls looked up and smiled.

"Thanks, aren't you a gentleman," she flirted.

Thea squeezed his hand. Valarie, how she hadn't missed her.

"You're welcome. Not enough room for me as well as all of you," was all he replied. He went to move on.

Valarie hadn't moved. Her three friends stood behind her waiting like patient little hounds.

"So, I didn't catch your name," she tried to sound sultry. He sighed and rolled his eyes before turning back to face her.

"I didn't give it," he faked a smile at her. She did her fake, flirty laugh.

"Well, I am Valarie, and luckily for you, you can have my number." She held out her perfectly manicured hand, holding a card.

"Look, love, I'm sure you're nice and all but you're not my type." Taken aback, she took an audible breath in. "Plus, I'm kind of seeing someone, sorry." He turned and walked away, pulling his hand, still holding Thea's, around to the front of him. He stroked his thumb over the top of her hand.

She was so stunned, she felt numb. Never had she ever seen Valarie so insulted. She wanted to roar with laugher, but she was just too shocked.

They rounded the corner and Ryder dropped the spell once more. He looked at Thea's stunned face.

"Look, I'm really sorry. I didn't mean to say I was seeing anyone, as I'm not, plus she seemed really annoying. I got the feeling from your death grip that you didn't like her, so I thought I would knock her down a peg or two, so yeah, I'm sorry," he blurted out and took a deep breath. Thea beamed at him.

"Ryder, that was bloody amazing. Never have I seen Valarie's face go so red before. You're the best." She flung her arms around his neck. He breathed out and hugged her back. They let the hug last a little longer than it really needed to. Thea took a tiny step back, nerves flooded her, and she knew it must show. He pushed her hair back from her cheek.

"You're really pretty, you know?" he complimented her. She just looked down, "Oh, come on; you can't be shy," he teased her. She squirmed.

"I'm nothing compared to Valarie back there. I'm plain and frankly a little bit boring," she mumbled. Ryder lifted her chin and made her look up at him.

"I don't like fake people. That girl wore enough makeup to put Barbie to shame, she was practically orange with all the fake tan, and finally, the clothes she was wearing! Surely her feet hurt in those heels! There is only so much pink anyone should wear at one time," he stated as a matter of fact.

Thea was in fits of laughter once again, but before she could answer him, he leaned down and planted a sweet little kiss upon her lips, which stole her breath away.

"Let's go before it gets too dark," he beamed at her and took hold of her hand once again.

Thea's house came into view no more than ten minutes later. She pointed out which one it was from the top of the street.

"Number five is mine," she said with her arm stretched out, pointing towards her house. "Why is the hallway light on upstairs?"

"Thea, wait!" He pulled her back. "Let me check." He closed his eyes and held his free hand out. His head bent slightly towards the ground, and his face wore a mask of pure concentration.

"Go, we need to leave quickly. I will hide you. Just go," Ryder sounded so panicked,

"What's wrong? Who's in my house? I thought no one could get in unless we said so?" she asked, but he was already dragging her back the way they came.

"I'm going to have to try and hide both of us," he said. "It costs a lot of energy, so if it's okay with you; can I syphon some of yours?" he asked her.

"Can you do what? … Wait, it doesn't matter. Just do it! Will it hurt?" she asked.

"It won't hurt. You might just feel a little tired," he said as they started to half walk, half run back down the street. "Here goes," he whispered.

Thea felt a slightly warm tingle run up her arm. She looked over at him as they hustled along; sweat was forming in little beads on his forehead. She wished she could help him. He was doing all the work, and she felt useless; she didn't know anything that would help. She was frustrated and annoyed at herself, there he was, trying to protect them both and she was just watching him struggle.

Deep down, something stirred within her. It felt hot as it built up in magnitude. She had no idea how she knew, but she focused on Ryder, the way he looked, the way he felt and smelt, everything about him. She felt like she was becoming one with him. Slowly she pushed the hot feeling within her over to Ryder. It must be working coz he instantly whipped his head round towards her. The sweat had disappeared, and his eyes seemed to glow with a new light.

"Thea, are you doing this?" he murmured to her.

"I think so. I needed to help you; you can't take this all on yourself," she answered.

"Thank you," he smiled. They ran the rest of the way back to the tunnel before dropping the shield. Both of them had their hands on their knees, breathing hard. When they finally stopped, Ryder was the first to speak.

"You're amazing," he laughed. "How on earth did you do that?" he questioned. "Never have I felt such power before; I felt as if I could do anything," he told her.

"I don't know. I just felt it there and somehow knew what to do with it," she confessed.

He grinned at her, his eyes shining. The next thing she knew he had grabbed her and pulled her close to him. She was fully embraced in his arms when he bent his head and kissed her. Never had she felt anything like it. So unexpected, but so wanted. She sank into the kiss, letting him whisk her away to a place she had never been before. Neither of them could catch their breath when they reluctantly pulled away.

Ryder rested his forehead on hers and just stood there with her in his arms for a bit. Thea didn't want this moment to end; it just felt so right.

"We better get back," he sighed before kissing her head. Thea looked up at him, hoping she didn't look all doe-eyed and stupid. Reaching down, Ryder laced his fingers with hers once more and pulled the dark tunnel door open.

"I'm sorry we didn't get into your house," he apologised.

"Who was in there?" she asked. Ryder was silent for a while. "Ryder?" she urged him. He let out a deep breath.

"My old coven," he finally told her.

"What! I thought you didn't know who your old coven was?" she reminded him.

"I know, I know, it's just, they're not the best people, and I didn't want to be judged by their actions; it's not fair. I don't want to be like them." His face had fallen; he stared at the ground, anywhere but at Thea.

"I won't judge you, Ryder." She placed her hand on his arm. "You can trust me."

He looked at her and took a deep breath; "I'm from the Nightshade coven." He let the words fall from his mouth. "I guess you have at least heard of them?" he asked her.

"Well, Margret said something about them in passing, but she wouldn't talk about them really," she said. "Why? What is so bad about them?" she waited for his answer.

"Ha, what is right about them?" his voice was full of loathing. Thea's face was blank. "You really have no clue? Wow, your mum did a good job keeping our world hidden from you," he sounded amused,

"Hey, it's not funny I feel totally lost and stupid," she said in pretend anger.

"Okay then, I'll give you the history lesson that you have been denied, but we have to walk and learn, okay?" Ryder smiled at her, and she nodded.

"A very, very long time ago, there was only one coven of witches, not the three main covens with lots of smaller covens everywhere, just one very big one," he began. "The leader of the coven was a witch called Julia, apparently she was kind and fair." He paused. "Not all the coven liked Julia's calm, gentle ways. Some wanted to overthrow her, and they felt the coven needed a fiercer, get the job done kind of person," he said.

"Now this is where it gets interesting, you see, one of the people who wanted the job was a guy called James." He looked at her waiting for any kind of reaction – he got nothing. "Okay, well he had a special ability, he could control all four elements and communicate with them." Thea gasped. "Finally, a reaction." Ryder laughed. "So yeah, James wanted the coven to follow him, so the coven was divided. Julia didn't like the idea of the coven being split, but James had gotten quite a big following," he continued. "So when the time came to vote, there was a third of the coven behind James. Julia thought she was safe with two thirds of the coven backing her but she was wrong; there was a large group that didn't agree with either Julia or James, and they formed a group of their own," he said.

"So, as you can see, they agreed to split into three separate covens, which was fine for a while. They all went their own ways, and things were fine," Ryder said. "Over time, one coven in particular started to put our existence in danger. They sought out different ways to gain more power, more dangerous; dark ways." Ryder paused again. "Anyway, they were led by James, and their coven was named the Nightshade coven; he had begun to favour dark twisted magic over the pure magic of our world." Thea looked at Ryan at this.

"What do you mean?" she questioned

"Well, he found immense power in blood magic," Ryder told her. "Ever since James found out that the power you gain from blood is so potent, he refused to practice any other form of magic. You see, if you didn't agree with him, you had to leave, either by your own free will or by force," Ryder informed her. "But in truth, you were never really allowed to leave, not fully. You could try, but in time you would be hunted down and either killed or captured." Sorrow filled his voice. "Plus, if a member of one of the other two covens found out who you were or where you were from, they were not much kinder to you either, so you were pretty stuck, really." He looked at Thea again; she looked beautiful walking next to him, taking in everything he said.

"So, what happened next? How come the Nightshade coven is hardly heard from any more?" Ryder looked at her

"Well, James had forsaken the old ways, he shunned anyone who didn't want to move forward with him, he fully changed himself, no longer was he a man of power, a mortal being, he had morphed himself into something new." He spoke, but it was as if he was no longer in the room with her. "A new kind of warlock was born through James, a hybrid of such." The tension in the room was so thick. "When you are born into the Nightshade coven, you are taught that it is a great honour to ascend to the higher form, but you can only do this after two important things have happened. One, you must have an heir, so you must have a child to carry on your name and lineage as the Nightshades do not take new people into the coven; only the original families are in the coven."

Thea was anxious; she felt a weird sense of importance in everything Ryder was saying.

"Two, you had to kill someone of equal power to yourself; and from one of the other two original covens, hence the hate towards the Nightshades." He sheepishly smiled at Thea.

"Do you have to do this Ryder?" she asked him, a bit scared of the answer.

"If I want to be a full member of the coven, then yes," he answered plainly. "But I left; I don't agree with their ways. I'm not like them," he hastened to add. "My father ascended about ten years ago. I have grown watching him gain his power. It changed him into something I no longer knew." Ryder sounded so sad. "My father's best friend has never ascended though," he told Thea.

"Does he not want to? Is he like you?" she asked him.

"No, he wants to ascend badly, he has tried to have a child with many different people, but it never seems to happen. He has killed loads of witches as powerful as him as well; he is bloody ruthless." Ryder took a deep breath. "My mother thinks it could be the fact that most male Nightshade warlocks can only sire one child. My mother thinks Aren has already sired a child, but no one knows where the child is." He stopped.

"You have to drink some of your child's blood to complete the ascension." She just looked at him. "All the children of our coven have been DNA tested; none of the children are his. There were whispers years ago that Aren had an affair with a witch from a rival coven, and she had gotten pregnant with his child. No one can find the witch or the child." Thea's blood ran cold as Ryder spoke. "Aren won't admit it as it is against the law to have relations with anyone outside the coven unless consented by the leaders, but a few people secretly knew Aren has been searching for the witch and child for a good few years now," he concluded. "So there you have it, my coven is twisted and cruel, and I wish to have nothing more to do with them. I didn't agree with their ways and left, the other covens don't need to know, or I'll be exiled or worse," he told her. He secretly hoped he could trust her.

"Your parents didn't care about taking your blood?" was the first thing Thea asked him. She was in pure shock, if she was honest, she didn't want to think too much about what she had just learnt.

"No, they wanted the power; they're like the rest now, higher beings they like to call themselves, when in fact they are actually a mix of witch and vampire. They need to drink blood on a regular basis to keep the power flowing strongly," he told her. "Pretty gross, huh, you can understand why I wanted out." She nodded, but in reality, she just felt numb.

Chapter 6

It was pretty late by the time Thea had gotten back to her room and she found her mum frantically pacing. She knew she shouldn't have stayed away so long, but she just couldn't bring herself to confront her mother. She knew she had to, even if just to eliminate the idea from her mind.

"Where the heck have you been, young lady?" her mum barely had control of her voice, the volume was off the scale.

"I know it's late and I'm sorry," Thea tried to apologise to her mum, but she knew it was going to take a lot more than a simple sorry for scaring her the way she had.

"Oh sure, you're sorry, great Thea, great, thank you so much for your apology. It makes the hours of worry so much better," her mum's voice was so sarcastic.

"I said I was sorry, mum. What else do you want me to say?" she was beginning to get annoyed too.

"Well, for one, you can explain where you have been, and why no one could find you, oh and how about you tell me about this new little friend I had to find out about from another person! I'm assuming that's his!" her mum paused as she pointed at the jacket. She sounded exasperated, "Secrets and lies, Thea, you know how much I hate them." Thea was about to explode at hearing her mum accusing her of secrets and lies.

"Well, that's rich, mother, seeing as my whole life has been one great big lie covered in thousands of secrets, so don't you go throwing morals at me that you do not even have yourself," the anger in Thea's voice was unavoidable, the look on her mum's face was pure shock, followed by deep sadness.

"You're right. I am the one that should be sorry, I tried to protect you, but instead, I may have put you in more danger," her mum admitted.

"I need the truth, mum," Thea spoke very quietly. "I have heard a lot in the last couple of hours. I need some answers from you. I need to understand everything," she continued. Thea knew she was making her mum feel uncomfortable; she felt incredibly nervous herself. "The Nightshade coven," she paused, looking at her mum, whose eyes had kind of glazed over. She could see the tears forming there. Thea's heart pumped faster. "They were at our house tonight before you ask, yes, I was there, and no, I was not seen," she stopped her mum from interrupting. "I don't know if they were there for me, you or something else," she ploughed on. "But, if it was me, then I need to know!" she said, leaving no room for her mum to wiggle her way out. She took a breath.

"I learned a name tonight," she told her. "Does the name Aren mean anything to you?" Thea asked. The unmistakable look of recognition, fear and something else showed as clear as day on her mother's face. Thea watched her mother closely; she was having trouble forming an answer. "I'll take your stunned silence and that look on your face as a yes; shall I?" she answered for her. A tear slipped from her mother's eye and ran down her cheek. "Do I even need to ask how you know him?" she looked at her and she felt sorry for her mother, but she was angry. Her whole life she had wondered who her father was, even asking about him a few times, getting shot down with numerous explanations that all turned out to be lies.

Free-flowing tears fell down her mother's cheeks; she had nothing to say to her daughter that Thea hadn't already worked out for herself. Her worst fear had come to pass and she was terrified for her child. Thea wasn't prepared for what knowing the name of her father would bring her.

"Rumour has it that Aren is looking for his child. I'm assuming I'm that child?" she finally said the words out loud. "Do you know why he's looking for me?" she asked her mum. She needed to know if what Ryder said was widely known. Her mum looked up at her through teary eyes.

"Yes, I believe so, darling. I'm so sorry, I never meant for you to find out about any of this. I was hoping to protect you for your whole life; I was stupid to think I could do that. Now I just hope we have time to prepare you just in case," she whispered.

Thea didn't know what to feel or what to say; she just stood there staring at the woman she called mother, the woman she loved more than any other but also the woman who lied to her.

"I need to think. I'll be back later, don't worry, I'll stay within the grounds," Thea reassured her.

Wandering the Halls of the buildings the Brockmoor witches called home had become a hobby to Thea. She had only been there a week yet she hadn't seen the whole place. The enchantment placed around it was very impressive. It really did just look like abandoned factories and housing from the outside. But on the inside, it was magnificent. The whole place was in fact a small estate, consisting of around eight separate buildings. The majority of the Brockmoor witches lived within its confines.

The children and young members of the coven all learned within its walls, inside the school the witches had created for them. They called it their safe haven from the outside world. Thea hadn't had any lessons as of yet with any other student; she was still solo learning.

She walked aimlessly around the estate. Looking for a place

to allow herself to just crash and sink into the tangled mess of thoughts.

Finally, she knew who her father was, what his name was and that he was still around. She didn't know how she felt about it, though. She was mad at her mum for the years of lies and secrets, but she also understood why she did it. She felt completely alone for the very first time. In the space of one short week her whole life had turned upside down. She had gone from being a normal girl turning seventeen, to a powerful witch who was being hunted for reasons unknown. She missed her old life and the one friend she had ever truly made. She missed her room and her own things.

Turning a corner, Thea came upon a set of stone steps leading down to an old-looking, bolted wooden door. Normally this would pique her interest, but today she just flopped down on the top step and wrapped her arms around her knees. She sat there a while just thinking when the hairs on the back of her neck began to tingle. It was the feeling she got when she felt someone was watching her. She wasn't afraid, and she didn't get the feeling of danger, just someone was there. Looking up, she saw Ryder closing the gap between them, and he sat down next to her.

"I see you found my favourite thinking spot too, huh?" he nudged her; she looked over to him, sighed and tried to give him a half-smile.

"How about hugging me instead… not that your knees aren't great or anything; I'm just sure my hugs are better," he joked as he put his arm around her shoulder and pulled her closer. She leaned into him and laughed a little, which quickly turned to sobs.

"Hey, whoa there, I didn't mean to make you cry," he said as he reached over to wipe a falling tear from her cheek.

He really was something to look at. Even though Thea felt

her life was falling apart, she couldn't help but take in his blond hair and stunning eyes. He smiled at her and ran his fingers through her hair.

"Come here," he whispered as he pulled her onto his lap for a proper cuddle. Thea was slightly startled, but it was greatly needed. She draped her arms around his neck and laid her head on his shoulder. She let the tears fall as he ran his fingers up and down her back.

"You're not alone, I know it's a lot to get used to and it's scary, but I promise; you're not alone," he reassured her. They sat like that for a while, him soothing her and her letting all the stress go. It wasn't long before Ryder realised he had a sleeping girl on his lap. He didn't want to wake her, but it was getting cold outside.

He was so much stronger than he looked. He stood up with ease with her still in his arms; she didn't even stir. Her head did roll slightly but came to rest with her lips just touching his neck. Tingles ran down his skin where they touched him.

"You do crazy things to me, Thea Jameson, and I have only just met you," he mumbled as he snuggled her closer and carried her inside.

The short walk to the guest wing didn't take Ryder long; he secretly wished it had taken longer. He didn't really want to put her down; he liked to be near her. She made him feel calm, as if there was a purpose to his life once more. He couldn't explain it, but it felt like he was meant to be around her, involved with her somehow. He hadn't meant to kiss her earlier, not that he didn't want to, but he should have held himself back. She had way too much to deal with as it was without him putting himself into the equation. Let alone the fact that he didn't want to have any real attachments. If any of his old coven found him, and found out how he felt for Thea, they would use her against him. He couldn't bear to think of that.

He had kept everyone at arm's length for years now, then this girl walked into his life, and within a week, he was hooked on her, yet she hadn't really done anything. He couldn't understand it; what he did know, though, was he wasn't going to let anyone harm her, not whilst he was around.

They came to Thea's room; the door was, of course, locked. Thea had mentioned her mother had a thing with waiting up for her in the adjoining room. He manoeuvred her around so that he could quietly knock on the door. Mere seconds had passed when the door flew open. Her mum looked just like her, just older. He couldn't help but stare at her.

"Thea, oh my goodness, is she okay?" her mum was frantic.

"She's fine Ms Jameson. She's just asleep." Ryder told her.

"Who are you?" she questioned him. "I'm a friend of Thea's, my name is Ryder," he smiled his half-smile. "I'm just going to lay her on the bed; she's been through a lot today and just needs sleep," he said as he walked to the bed and gently laid her down, sliding his arms out from beneath her.

"Thanks for bringing her back," her mum said as she held the door. She wanted to question him more about who he was and why he was around her daughter so much, but she let it slide for now. He was right; her daughter had been through enough for one day.

He turned to leave.

"Ryder," Thea called to him. Turning around, he sat on the side of the bed next to her

"I'm still here," he murmured.

"Stay with me, don't go yet," she was so tired, but she wasn't letting him go. She felt like she needed him tonight. She pleaded

78

him as she clasped her fingers with his. Her mum saw the whole thing. How their hands intertwined and how she called for him as soon as he let her go. Ryder looked up at Ellen, he didn't want to leave, but he couldn't stay if Thea's mum was going to have a problem.

"It's fine, Ryder, you can stay… no funny business though, okay?" she smiled at him. She knew right now she had to do what her daughter wanted and needed. Clearly, she needed this boy, and it pained her that Thea hadn't called for her, but she understood how it was. "I'll be right next door if you need me okay? And remember, no funny business! I will know," she said, making herself abundantly clear.

"Of course, Ms Jameson, thank you," Ryder answered. He reached over and stroked Thea's cheek, and grinned. "Move over, make me some room," he nudged her along and sat beside her with his long legs stretched out down the length of the bed. He wrapped his arm around her shoulder and pulled her closer. "Time to sleep, pretty girl. I'll be right here all night, I promise," he kissed her forehead and closed his eyes.

Thea's world was totally insane; the last thing she remembered was sitting on the steps outside somewhere and crying herself silly with Ryder.

"On his lap… oh my lord… I was sat in his arms crying like a fool," she couldn't believe herself. Thea sat bolt upright in her bed; everything came rushing back. She remembered him staying the night with her, all because she had asked him to. She looked around, searching for him, he wasn't there, and her stomach sank. There was a soft knock at her door. Her mum stuck her head round and smiled at her daughter,

"Don't worry, love, he just popped out. He was summoned for something," she told her. "He was very insistent that he would be back," she finished.

"Okay, thanks, Mum, not that I'm worried or anything, I just wondered, you know," she tried to convince her, or was she really trying to convince herself.

"Yeah, I know, love, but he is cute, though," her mum chided.

"Oh Mum, please no," Thea found herself laughing, something she didn't think she would be doing for a long time, let alone with her mother.

"Come on, Thea, he is, and so sweet and charming, very caring towards you last night," her mum carried on

"Really? Was he?" Thea couldn't help herself asking.

"Yes, he carried you all the way here and wouldn't let you go until he was happy you were safe, and as soon as you called out to him, he was there like a shot," her mum was really enjoying herself getting to tell Thea about last night's antics. "And once I agreed he could stay, well he climbed right up on the bed with you and wrapped his arm around you, even kissed your head," she made swooning noises, embarrassing her daughter all the more.

"Whoa, hold up, Mum. How do you know? Were you spying on us?" Thea tried and failed to look stern. A stupidly big grin plastered itself firmly on her face.

"No, no, nothing like that. I was just checking that no silly business was going on," she laughed back. "He seems like a nice boy Thea. I approve… for now," she winked at her daughter.

"Yay, Mummy approves. Hmmm, now I'm not so sure if I like him," she joked back.

"Ouch, and I thought I had won half the battle charming your mum," Ryder said as he slipped in through the half-open door.

Thea's face was instantly red. He couldn't help but laugh at

80

her.

"See, that face is irresistible," he said as he went to kiss the top of her head.

"Ryder, my mum is right there," Thea was so embarrassed she didn't know what to do with herself.

"Don't worry, I am leaving now. I have business to attend too, and I'll see you two love birds later," she waved at them as she left. Thea was worse than stunned. Her mum was being totally cool about a boy staying the night with her, and the boy she liked seemed to like her back.

"What is this world coming to?" she thought she had said to herself, but apparently, it was out loud.

"I know, right? Totally crazy," Ryder replied. He sat grinning at her as he took her hand. "How you feeling today?" he asked her as his thumb traced circles across the top of her hand. Electricity was racing through her body every time his thumb rubbed over her skin.

"Umm, I feel bewildered, lost, very confused, extremely embarrassed and hungry," she hid her face with her one free hand.

"There's no need to be embarrassed with me, Thea, I swear," he tried reassuring her. "Plus, I get the lost and confused feeling too, well... and the hungry," he laughed at his joke.

"Umm, so thanks for staying with me last night," she said; the words kind of fell out of her mouth a bit too fast, sounding all jumbled.

"No problem, to be honest, I'm glad I got to stay. I didn't really want to leave," he admitted. This time it was his turn to be red-faced. "I would have missed that awkward talk with your mum; you know about me and how cute you look with your morning hair," he teased her

"Oh, hell no," Thea threw her hands up to her head, trying

to tame the tangled mess that was her hair. All the while Ryder laughed at her

"I think I might have found a new hobby," he laughed. "You're so funny to wind up." She stuck her tongue out and launched herself at him. He was too quick for her, though, and caught her before she even reached him.

"Struggling is futile, Miss Jameson. You are mine now," he said in his best villain voice.

"I surrender, I surrender," Thea squeaked at him; she could hardly breathe. "So, what do we do now?" she asked him once she had finally calmed down.

"Well, first we get you some food, then I think it's best if we get you some training. I know you're going to need it," he said to her, all trace of play gone; now he meant business. "I wish I could teach you, but I'm meant to not know a lot of magic. If I admit that I lied, then they'll be on me like a rash. I hope you understand," he paused

"It's okay, don't worry. I'll go and see Jo, I'm sure she can help," Thea said. "But Ryder, could you stay nearby?" she asked him.

"Of course I will," he smiled. "I won't leave you, remember? I promised you last night!"

Chapter 7

The weather seemed to mimic Thea's mood. One minute it was clear, the next it was pouring with rain. No one could understand what was going on. They all said it was magically charged. Thea had quite the shock that morning, not just remembering everything with Ryder but also one of her elemental friends paid her a visit without being summoned.

She was in the bathroom getting ready to leave when her arms began to tingle. She looked down from brushing her teeth to see a small flame sliding up and down her left arm. She almost screamed until she heard his tiny voice inside her mind. He told her not to be scared; they meant her no harm. They had sent him to inform her that something big was coming; they could feel it. They seemed to like having a human to talk to once again, one that wasn't crazy, or so they said. Thea was convinced she was going crazy; so she wasn't so sure how long her new little friends would stick around.

She finished what she was doing and then asked the flame what to do next. But he was already gone. She looked around the room for him, thinking he might have just moved, but he was really gone. She left the room and found Ryder waiting for her.

"Ready, princess?" he spoke without looking up. He was busy fiddling with something small in his hand.

"Uh, yeah," she replied distantly.

"You okay?" he asked her while putting the thing back into his pocket.

"Yeah, honestly, I'm okay, just a bit confused. The flame element spoke to me again in the bathroom. He said there was something big going to happen; that they could feel it," she relayed. "Then he was just gone like he hadn't been there at all." Ryder rushed over to her and grabbed her by the shoulders; she could feel his touch all the way to her skin, even through her new black leather jacket.

"Whoa, is everything okay? Are you okay?" he was genuinely concerned.

"Honestly, I'm fine. Maybe I'm going crazy, who knows?" she said as she shook her head. "Come on, let's go."

Ryder took her hand as soon as they left the room. He had no intention of losing sight of her; not even once. He had made her a promise that he would stay close, and that was exactly what he planned to do. Thea loved it, so she really didn't mind. She did mind the dirty looks she got from a few of the other girls they passed on the way to find Jo, though. Ryder sensed her unease.

"What's wrong, beautiful?" he asked playfully.

"It's weird, don't you think? I haven't seen anyone around these halls for days, but now they're packed with people, and a lot of the girls seem to hate me," she voiced

"Well, you see, because you were new and none of the elders knew what you were capable of, they shut this wing off to all the other students until they knew more about you," he answered.

"Okay, fine! That clears that bit up, but what about the girls' death glares," she pointed out. He shifted from one foot to the other.

"Umm, that's my fault, really," he confessed. "Well, you see, umm, since I have been here, practically all the girls have asked me out or something of the sorts, and I have turned every single one down," he looked at her sheepishly.

"Oh, wow, so I'm hated because they fancy you?" she laughed. "Brilliant, I'm dating the most wanted guy in school. I'm honoured," she said with air quotations; she laughed out loud.

He pulled her to a stop and pressed her gently up against the wall, pinning her there with his body, making her look up at him and taking her breath away; it always did when he looked at her like that.

"So, we are dating, are we?" he grinned in such a playful way and leaned in closer. She could feel her face going red.

"Umm, I just thought because of all, you know," she babbled. She felt mortified. Had she jumped to conclusions? He laughed out loud

"Shut up silly and come here. He leaned down and planted a kiss right on her lips for everyone to see," when he pulled away, he whispered in her ear, "I have wanted to do that all morning, and yes, we are dating. I will be telling everyone you're my girlfriend, so to back off; he kissed her cheek and laughed. "You okay with that?" she was breathless. All she could do was nod and hope she didn't look as stupid as she felt. "Oops, sorry, don't look now, but I think they saw that; judging by their faces, I think I might have made you some more enemies," he chuckled into her hair.

"You're lucky you're so hot," she told him playfully, finally finding her voice again. Ryder straightened up, took Thea's hand once more and pulled her along with him. He slowed as he passed a group of girls and smiled at them.

"All right, ladies?" he said as he went passed them, leading Thea with him. He squeezed her hand and carried on.

"Ow, you're wicked, aren't you?" she laughed. She couldn't help it, never had she been the one with the hot guy; she was always the one left dreaming.

Jo's office door was open when they arrived; Ryder slowed them before they were seen. Voices could be heard drifting out of the room.

"What do you mean I have to up the training now? How do I train a kid with no background knowledge whatsoever in magical attack and defence?" Jo's voice floated through the door.

"They have been spotted and sensed closer to us than they have been for a very long time," replied what Thea thought was Daniel's voice.

"So? that doesn't mean I can teach any faster than she can learn just because they are closer now; I'm not a miracle worker," Jo spat back, a little louder this time.

"I have been told that both Thea and Ryder went off together yesterday afternoon without telling anyone. We need to find out if either of them saw anything, and more importantly, if they were seen themselves." A new voice joined the conversation.

"Yes, you are right. We will get right on it," Daniel replied.

"Ryder, what do we do? They are talking about us," Thea said.

"Don't worry, it's okay; we will get through this together, I promise. Now let's get in there before anything gets worse," he finished.

"Speak thy name, and thy shall appear," Jo said quite loudly. "Thea, Ryder, you may come in now," she called out to them. Thea went rigid and Ryder led her in. "I assume you heard all of that," she addressed them. Standing in front of them were Jo, Daniel and the new leader of the Brockmoor coven.

"We heard enough, yes," Ryder did the speaking. "What is it you intend us to do? And what do you want to know from us?" he asked.

"Ryder, my dear boy, this is not an interrogation, so do not act so threatened. We will not harm either of you," Grace replied. "We just want to know if you were seen and what you saw, like you heard us say before," she told him.

"No, we were not seen, I made sure of it. I may not know who I am, but I still remember how to do a basic cloaking spell," he told them. He still had hold of Thea's hand. She was clutching it for dear life. He wasn't sure if he would have any blood flowing to his fingers if she held on any tighter.

"Okay, so what did you see, if you don't mind me asking?" Grace asked him. "Don't worry, neither of you will get in any trouble; we just need to know whatever we can, so we can be ready for whatever we might be up against," she concluded. Daniel turned to Thea

"How about, Thea, you go and talk with Jolene and Ryder can stay and talk to us?" he looked from Thea to Ryder. Thea clammed up harder; she didn't want to go anywhere without Ryder, she felt so strongly about staying with him. Jo sensed it right away; she knew they would get nowhere splitting them up. Jo touched her brother's shoulder.

"Dan, I think for now they should stay together! If you cannot sense the protectiveness these two have going on for each other, then something is wrong with you," she muttered to him while smiling at them.

"Yes, you are right as always, sister," he replied through gritted teeth. Thea physically relaxed, and Ryder started to trace circles on her hand once again, it soothed her and he knew it.

Jo looked at the pair of them for a while, summing up what she was going to ask very carefully. Thea was clearly stressed, and Ryder was barely keeping her together. It was easy to see he was coaching her through this situation; they had become incredibly close in a really short time.

"Ryder, first of all, why did you decide it was a good idea to sneak out in the first place? You knew there might be people looking for Thea?" Jo asked him. She couldn't understand why they would risk such a thing.

"Thea just wanted to get a few things from her house, Miss, she was missing home and wanted some home comforts," he replied very plainly. Thea nodded in agreement.

"Okay, when did you realise it was not safe to be there and leave? Were you seen at all?" she continued to ask.

"We didn't even get to the house. Thea saw a light on in her house from down the street and thought it was weird, so I did a sensor spell to determine who was in her house and if it was safe," he told her. His blood ran cold; he had just let on that he could do a high-level spell. They would know for sure now that he was more than he was letting on. He hid any expression from his face.

"Who was there, Ryder?" she urged him on.

"Four members of the Nightshade coven," Ryder answered without hesitation. "As soon as I knew who it was, I turned us around and we ran back here. We didn't even approach the house," he continued. "I'm pretty sure they couldn't sense my magic," he concluded.

"Yes, they would have! You stupid boy. They would have sensed the magic running through your veins before you even did the spell; they let you go," Daniel snapped at him, anger rolling off him in waves. "You have probably led them straight to us," he cursed.

"Dan, that's enough," Jo scolded. Ryder's face had paled at the idea of being found by his old coven. If he was found, then all hope was lost for him. Ryder suddenly dropped Thea's hand with a sudden intake of breath.

"Ouch, what was that?" Ryder held up his hand to see. All of his fingers, including his thumb, had been burnt. He looked at Thea. She was staring at her hand

"Ryder, I'm so sorry I didn't mean to burn you; in fact, I didn't even know I was doing anything," she confessed in a panic. A tiny flame sprang to life on her fingertips, making the whole room jump. They all looked from Thea to her hand, then back to her again.

"What's going on?" Ryder asked her

"Uh, my little friend here wanted to be heard," Thea stumbled over the words.

"Well, what does he have to say then?" Grace asked, a little impatient.

"I am Zans, and I come bearing a warning for you all, dark things are on the rise, and you would be wise to do right by this child. We have taken it upon ourselves to teach her the old ways; she is very gifted and has been chosen to bear the task of cleansing the magical world. Choose your ways wisely, for you do not know the true weight of your decisions," Thea's voice spoke for the tiny flame. The whole room was stunned. Thea took a short, sharp breath and then collapsed to the floor. Ryder dropped to his knees instantly and was by her side.

"Thea? Thea, can you hear me?" he called. He was scared, and panic surged through him. "What have I just witnessed?" he thought as he tried to help the girl he was rapidly falling for. Jo stood up; she had knelt beside Thea too.

"She will be fine; she is just sleeping. Channelling an elemental being will be very tasking," she informed them. Grace cleared her throat,

"Sounds like this is much bigger than we first thought.

History is in the making here," she said breathlessly. "I think it's about time you tell us who you truly are, young man, and how you knew who those people in Thea's house were, as it may very well help our cause," Grace directed her words to Ryder.

Ryder spent the rest of the morning trying his best to explain himself and his situation to the elders, the whole time worrying about Thea.

Naturally, Daniel was furious with him, and he wanted Ryder put under twenty-four-hour supervision. He had lied to the whole coven so convincingly for a long time.

"How can you all be so calm about this? This boy is a member of the Nightshade coven, yet you are willing to just let him carry on walking around here like it is nothing," Daniel practically spat at them. "He is most probably a spy for them; who knows how much information on us he has already fed back to them," Daniel glared at Ryder.

"For the tenth time, I'm not a spy," Ryder yelled. He was getting tired of all the judgemental comments. He had only agreed to talk about himself as he knew it directly affected Thea.

"Everyone, calm down. All this shouting will get us nowhere," Grace spoke up.

"Ryder, will you consent to a mind-reading test?" she asked him. "It will clear up any misunderstandings as well as clarify who you are," she spoke with ease; not an ounce of tension was in her voice. Ryder tensed from head to toe, though. Mind-reading as such was harmless and painless. But a mind-reading test was something altogether different. He looked over at the sleeping girl; he knew what he felt was much more than infatuation. He thought about how he so desperately wanted to get to know her better, to spend time with her, laughing and joking and basically just having fun. He sighed; he wanted to do all the normal things people do when they first fall in love. He was silently stunned as he realised he might very well be falling in love with this girl he hardly knew, yet he knew he would move heaven and earth for her.

"Yes, I consent to whatever tests you want me to do," he said as he continued to stare at Thea's sleeping form.

"Very well then," Grace smiled, her hands folded neatly in front of her. "Jolene, would you kindly perform the test now, please?" she looked Jo's way.

"Ma'am, normally we give the person in question twenty-four hours to prepare for such an intrusive test," she pointed out.

"Yes, I am well aware of the normal protocol, dear, but this is not a normal case. We need to clear this up now so we can prepare for what is to come," Grace left no room for discussion. Jo nodded and stepped over to Ryder. Sorrow swam in her dark brown eyes. She truly was sorry for how this was going.

"It's okay, Jo, just get it done," Ryder smiled and tried to look at ease, for Jo's sake at least. She had been so kind to him when he first came to the coven; in fact, she was one of the only people he truly liked here.

Ryder was sat in the very middle of the room. Everyone else had moved to the far sides, out of Jolene's way.

"Ryder, I am going to reach into your mind quite forcefully, I'm afraid. So, prepare yourself, I do apologise, but this isn't going to be pleasant," Jo declared before taking a sharp breath in. She closed her eyes and reached out with one hand towards Ryder. He was sat stock still; he hardly dared to breathe, waiting for the searing pain to pierce through his head. A couple of moments passed with nothing happening; Ryder began to relax. Before he knew what had hit him, though, he was in complete agony. It was as if someone had stabbed into his mind with a burning hot poker and was scraping around for hidden objects.

All his memories came flashing by in front of his eyes, every single one from the earliest to the most recent. He heard a scream, unsure if it was part of an old memory; or him, unable to hold his voice throughout the ordeal. Frankly, he didn't care. Images of his mother slammed into his mind; he loved her yet loathed her at the same time. She allowed his father to treat him as though he was a means to an end. He never cared for Ryder; he just needed him there so that he could ascend. His mother, though, he was sure she cared for him. Pain ripped through his heart, pain he had locked away for a very long time came rushing back with a vengeance, and he could hardly breathe.

His body shook as memory after memory assaulted his mind. He had worked so hard to lock that painful part of his life away; deep inside his mind where he couldn't see it, think of it or hardly even remember it. Finally, the bombardment of images slowed down. They slowed to show how he chose to leave his old coven, how hard it was to get away from them and his struggle to find places to stay, to be safe. Jo lingered on the memory of how it was her and Dan who had stumbled across him, and how they had encouraged him to come back to the Brockmoor compound with them.

Jo could feel how he had felt. She could see and feel that it was tricks and lies that had gotten him where he wanted to be, like Dan had suspected of him, but fear mixed with relief. She eventually moved past this image and cycled through the most recent memory. Ninety percent of them were about Thea; he felt uncomfortable sharing his feelings and thoughts of her with Jo, they were still so new to him, but right now he really didn't have a choice. Finally, the burning pain was lifted from his mind. He was left with a dull throbbing ache on either side of his head, his vision was blurry, and his throat was sore.

"He is telling the truth, Ma'am," Jo declared. She couldn't believe what Ryder had been through, not only now but throughout his whole life. She really felt for the boy.

"Ah, good, well now that is all cleared up, we can move on to more important things," Grace said with a smile.

"Let me go, Daniel. I swear you will regret it if you don't," Thea was seething with anger. She had woken up to the sounds of Ryder's tortured screams. It had ripped through her like a knife straight to her heart.

Ryder looked up. His hair dripped with sweat, his face was pale, he had nasty black circles around his eye, and his whole body trembled. He forced a smile her way.

"What on earth do you think you were going to achieve by torturing him?" she glared at them all.

"You say the Nightshades are bad, but right now you look no better," she shook Daniel's hands off her shoulders and shoved past him to kneel in front of Ryder.

"You know nothing of what you speak, little girl," Daniel shot back.

"Maybe I don't know a lot about the magic world, but I do know about human decency, and right now none of you have shown an ounce of it," Thea was shaking with anger.

"Now hold on right there, young lady," Margret piped in. She had entered just after Thea had passed out.

"No, you hold on. If you wanted answers from him, you could have gotten them in a much simpler way, but no, you went straight for the worst way possible, you preach about the wrongdoings of the Nightshade coven, yet you hear a mention of their names and you turn around and become barbaric." Thea stopped only to breathe. "If you claim to be better than them, then

I think you should start acting like it, because right now you're doing a pretty poor job of proving to me that I will be safe with you," she finished. Anger hung in the air, mixed with guilt.

Grace had ordered a couple of people to help Ryder to his room after Thea's brutal speech. She had gone along with her very new and exhausted boyfriend. Refusing to leave his side.

Ellen popped her head in on the pair not long after they had arrived back. News had spread pretty fast of how Thea had shot down the top members of the council with her unforgiving tongue.

The council was going to have a hard time covering up the reason for Ryder's horrific screams, which had been heard all over the building. Ryder was laid out on his bed; he had tried to reassure Thea that it was okay, and he had agreed to the test. But she was having none of it. She didn't agree with that kind of treatment. And if they wanted anything from her, things would have to change.

"You okay, darling?" her mum's voice floated across the room.

"Yes, no, I don't know," she answered. Her mum hugged her from behind.

"Sounds like you had quite a time today, huh?" she said. Thea just sat there and eventually nodded. She was still so angry.

"He's on our side, Mum, I know it," she declared. "Heck, I don't even know what our side is," she let a little laugh slip out, followed by a strange little hiccup.

"I know, sweetheart, just know I am on your side too."

Chapter 8

The next couple of days were split between training with Jo and visiting Ryder. At first it was hard for Thea to train with Jo without being really mad at her. She trusted her, yet she had performed that test on her boyfriend. She loved saying that:

"Her boyfriend."

Eventually, she came to realise Jo was just doing her job, and she truly didn't want to hurt Ryder. She would get up extra early in the morning and rush to Ryder's room, and she totally disregarded the fact that Margret had said she wasn't allowed to be in his room on her own. Apparently, this was a rule for all students. She would spend around an hour cuddled up on his bed with him, just chatting about everything and anything. He was slowly getting better, but he still looked exhausted. He wasn't ready to talk about it yet so she didn't push it. Then she would rush off to meet Jo by the old grandfather clock to start her training for the day. It was really odd, though, as nothing more had happened. It was as if everyone was just waiting for someone to make the next move.

The entire council were on edge. They knew the Nightshades were close by, yet they hadn't shown themselves. Thea was learning all the different defensive moves and protective spells she would need to defend herself should she be attacked. She was learning much quicker than she was before. Now the elements were on her side and helping her along. She just seemed to pick it all up so much easier. She found herself doing moves that she didn't even know she could do, and she wasn't getting half as tired.

"That's enough for today, Thea," Jo called; she was the one who was actually tired.

"Okay, same time tomorrow?" Thea called back. She was keen to leave; to get back to Ryder before she was pulled away by Simon or Margret for more magical law and history.

She was dressed in her comfortable three-quarter length jogging bottoms and a black tank top. She had her hair tied back in a high ponytail. She knew she looked a mess, but she didn't care; she just needed to get back to him. Jo just nodded and carried on packing up her things.

She had been spending her mornings training Thea and her afternoons with her brother, searching the nearby buildings for any signs of Nightshade members. It was very late every night before Jo got back in. Daniel was insisting on double-checking everything and putting extra protection spells around the estate.

Walking along the now-quiet corridors to Ryder's room always felt as if it took forever. Thea kind of walked and ran at the same time. She finally turned the corner and saw his door was ajar.

"Hmm, that's odd? Normally he keeps the door fully shut." Walking slowly and quietly, she crept up to the door. She listened, hardly daring to breathe. She didn't want to miss anything.

"What do you know, tell me before anything is said to her," Ellen's voice drifted out of the door. She was using her hushed but urgent voice she only used when she was really nervous.

"Look, Ms Jameson, I don't know anything; I have told you everything I know already." Ryder sounded exasperated. "I had every single bit of information ripped from my mind already, you heard them do it," he pointed out.

"How did you know I was there?" she genuinely sounded shocked.

"Oh, come on, Ms Jameson, you know very well that we can sense our own, so don't try to play the fool with me, I may be young still, but I know my fair share of Nightshade law and history," he told her.

"Fine, Ryder, but please, the less Thea knows about my past right now, the better," she continued.

"How is that better? She is in danger for many reasons, and you know that," he paused. "Plus, no one has even spent a second thinking about your other coven, The Willow witches. They are just as bad as the Nightshades in a way," he concluded. Thea's head was spinning; her mother was in her boyfriend's room talking about keeping more secrets from her. She rested her back against the wall and tried to catch her breath; the world had begun to spin.

"Look, Ms Jameson, I respect you as one of my elders, but Thea means the world to me," he said. Thea couldn't believe what she was hearing; she was elated to hear how much she meant to him, yet terrified that things were happening behind her back. "Yes, I know we haven't known each other long, but you know yourself when you find the one; time isn't an issue," he barely took a breath before continuing, "so when it comes to Thea, I'm sorry, but I won't keep things from her, I won't lie to her, and I won't put her in danger. I will do anything else you ask of me if it will help; but if it means Thea could get hurt in any way, be it physically or emotionally, then no, I don't want any part in that," he said pointedly. Thea heard her mother audibly take a deep breath.

"You're right, Ryder. I'm sorry, I can't lie to her any more, even though it scares me to think she is in so much danger, I can no longer protect her." Time stretched on before her mum spoke again. "Help me protect her in every way you can, no one else knows how truly bad the Nightshades are, and the Willows, too," she got up to leave.

Thea heard the chair legs scrape along the floor, she had mere seconds to hide before her mum caught her listening in.

"Get well soon, Ryder. Thea is going to need you," she called out before closing the door behind her and walking back down the corridor.

Thump, thump, thump was the only sound Thea could hear, her heart was pounding so hard. The world had come to a standstill; time felt as if it had practically stopped when in fact only seconds had passed. She couldn't drag enough air into her lungs, no matter how hard she tried. Had she really heard that her mother was a member of the Nightshade coven as well as the Willow witches?

Thea looked up and found herself to be standing in Ryder's doorway, just staring at him. She could see his lips moving but couldn't hear the words. She hadn't even realised she had moved from her hiding spot.

"Thea, what's wrong? Why are you looking at me like that? What's happened?" Ryder's words suddenly hit her like a train slamming into her at full speed.

"Huh, what?" was her only reply. He got up from his bed and went to her.

"Tell me what has happened and how I can help?" he gently asked. He took in the expression on her face; she was so beautiful to him. He knew she didn't see what he saw, but that was part of the reason he liked her so much. Right now, her whole face was twisted in an odd mix of confusion, bewilderment, and a touch of fear. Gently, he ran his fingers through her hair, trying to tease any reaction from her. Thea eventually shook her head and looked him square in the eye.

"My mother was here talking to you," she finally said, his face paled before she finished.

"Let me explain," he said before she could say another word, but she continued regardless.

"She's a Nightshade coven member? And you knew?" a tear rolled down her cheek, out of anger or fear, she didn't know.

"Thea, it's not like that; I haven't known for long. I had a very small suspicion for a couple of days but only knew for sure this morning," he hoped she believed him. Losing her now would crush him. He had only just found her, he didn't want to lose her already.

"I heard what you said to my mum," she whispered while focusing on her feet.

"You did?" he was nervous. Thea nodded. She took a step forward and just rested her head on his chest. She never looked up or spoke, she just leaned into him. Instinctively he wrapped his arms tightly around her.

Relief flooded through Ryder, from his head to his toes. He had never been so scared to lose something so badly before. Even when his own life was in danger, he had not felt that kind of fear.

A couple of hours had passed since Thea arrived at his doorway. A lot of tears had been shed, and a lot of emotions lay bare. Both Thea and Ryder were exhausted. It took a lot out of her to open up to anyone as much as she had to him, and it took hardly anything to exhaust Ryder right now.

The moon had risen high in the sky by the time Thea decided she really should get going and face her mother, but she wanted so badly to stay.

"I better get going," she said as she heaved herself up. He

pulled her back down and kissed her.

"I wish you could stay," he grumbled into her hair. He made her insides melt in all the good ways.

"I know, I wish I could too, but I better go see my mum and get this over with," she confessed. He pulled his fake, sad face, which always made her laugh.

"Okay, beautiful, just remember I'm right here if you need me," he reminded her. She smiled; kissed him one last time; lingering a little too long on his lips, then pulled away and waved at the door. Moments like this made her love her new life until everything else that came with it came crashing back down.

As she walked back to her room she thought about her old life, her old school and Jason. She missed Jason. She wondered if he ever thought about her or if his mind had now been fully wiped of all things Thea. She grinned to herself, thinking what Valarie would look like if she saw Thea with Ryder.

"One day, when all this is over, I will have to make that image happen," she told herself with a laugh. Before she knew it, she stood outside her door, reluctant to go in. She knew her mum would be all nice and pleasant; she would ask her about her day and pretend that it was all okay.

"How am I meant to respond to that?" she puzzled. "Oh well, there's no time like the present."

Her mum was sitting reading, just like she thought. She looked up as Thea came in and smiled at her. She put her book down and stood to kiss her daughter on the head.

"Hello darling, I was just wondering when you would be back." Thea just stood there. "What's wrong, love? Has something happened?" Thea continued to just stand there. The silence was deafening. "For goodness' sake, Thea, speak to me," Ellen was losing her patience.

"You're a member of the Nightshade coven! When did you plan on telling me?" she glared at her mother. "Oh wait, you weren't! You only wanted to discuss it with my new, very weak, boyfriend behind my back!" she accused her; anger rolled off Thea like thunder. Thea could feel the energy, and yes it did scare her a little, but she couldn't stop it. "And before you accuse Ryder of tattling on you, he didn't. I was stood outside the room the whole time," she concluded. Her mother just stood there stunned. "So, go on then, Mum, spin me another tall tale to make it all okay for me, or should we say it as it is, it would make it easier for you," Thea continued. Ellen looked at her daughter. She had never seen her so mad before, never filled with so much anger, and it scared her.

"I'm not a true member of that coven, Thea. By birth, yes, but nothing more, you need to understand," she tried to tell her, but Thea had had enough of being pushed over and fobbed off.

"That's the thing, Mum, I don't understand because you keep on insisting that everything be kept from me! I'm not a little girl that you need to protect any more," she shot back at her. Thea's fists were clenched so tight her knuckles were white.

"Then let me at least explain it to you. If you want me to not treat you like a little girl, you have to give me the chance to tell my story," she spoke softly. "Yes, I was born to the Nightshade coven, both my parents were very respected members of the coven," she said. "My father was," she paused, "let's say he was very important, and my mother would do anything to please him." Thea relaxed a bit; she needed to concentrate on what her mum was saying. "My parents needed to have a child to progress up the ladder, so when they found out my mother was carrying a child, they were thrilled," she smiled. "But not like normal people would be excited, a child to the Nightshades is actually a means to an end, nothing more; it's very rare for a child to actually mean something to their parents. Most couples can only have one child. So, you wouldn't see a family with more than one unless they have twins, which are incredibly rare. But of course, my parents would have twins, wouldn't they? They always had to be the best," she spat

"Wait, Mum, you're a twin?" Thea was so shocked she had never heard even a whisper of a sibling from her mum.

Ellen sighed, "Yes, darling, I had a twin brother," she confirmed. "My brother was three minutes older than me and instantly the favoured child. Of course, my parents played up the 'we have twin's' thing as often as they could, but in truth, they didn't really care. They had my brother who was shining in everything he did; he was the golden child. They had the child they needed to ascend, and they also had the child that would be as successful as them." She paused. "You see, Eli was just like them in every way. He was clever and excelled in his magic training much better than me. I was just an annoyance to them, if truth be told."

Thea couldn't believe what she was hearing; her mum was so loving towards her. How could she have grown up so differently? She felt sorry for her.

"Anyway, when I turned fifteen, I'd had enough. My brother shone so brightly to everyone, not just my parents. It would soon be time for my parents to ascend, and seeing as they had two children, they could both use a different child, meaning their power wouldn't be weakened. They would be equally as powerful as each other." She looked up at Thea, making sure she was following all she was saying.

"You told me you were taken from your family at a really young age, and you didn't remember anything?" Thea pointed out.

Ellen looked down at her feet; the shame on her face was clear.

"I'm sorry, darling, that was a lie. I didn't want my true past coming to light," Thea just shook her head; lies were becoming the norm to her now.

Her mother took a deep breath and carried on. "Anyway, my brother was really keen to be part of the ascension, and I wasn't. I had spent my life being pushed around and treated like nothing, so when the opportunity arose for me to leave, well, I did. I took my chance and escaped. It wasn't long after that when the Willow witches found me and took me in," she concluded.

Thea just sat with her mouth hanging open. She hadn't been expecting that.

"Life was better for you once you joined the Willows though, yeah?" she asked her mum.

"For a while yes, but not always. You see, once a Willow witch, always a Willow witch. They will take you in and teach you their ways, but in return, you have to do everything you are told, and you are not allowed to leave," she sounded so miserable. "Basically, I had switched one hell for another. They had planned to raise me up as their own, like they do with many Witches they take in, and to them, I had a lot of power even though it didn't seem so to my family." She paused. "I was to be married off to one of their pure blood Willow coven members. They wanted to harness my power and pass it down through their bloodlines too. Once I found out their plan, I intended to leave once again," she told Thea. "I was sent on an errand one day, which took me a little too close to my old coven; they weren't aware, of course, though. I would never admit where I was truly from. By pure chance I bumped into your father, Aren. Something sparked inside me, and I was sure it was the same for both of us. I knew who he was but he didn't know me. You see, he was from a high-up family in the Nightshade coven," she was cut off by Thea asking questions.

"Didn't you say you were really important in the coven, though, surely he should know you?" she wondered.

"Well, yes, but I wasn't always included in important functions and things when I got a bit older; when I did get to do things, I was pretty much hidden away like I was an embarrassment or something," she clarified. "But when I met him after I had left, I was much older. He didn't recognise me, things were great. I stuck with my new coven purely because I wanted to see Aren; if I left them, I would have to run, and I would never see him again, so I stayed," she shrugged. "A couple of months went by and I was deeply in love with him. I thought he felt the same; it really seemed like it. But once I told him I was pregnant, he froze and refused to see me any more, our secret meetings ended, and I was left heartbroken and pregnant. I couldn't just up and leave then, not in my state; it would be too dangerous," Ellen looked her daughter in the eye. "I refused to allow my child to be brought into a world like I was raised in. I was going to love and protect my child at all costs. I would not be my mother."

Thea was shocked by her mum's story; never did she think her mum's life was like that. She had always painted it to be like a fairy tale or something similar.

"I love you, Mum," Thea declared. "You have done a lot for me that I never even realised you were doing, but now it is time for you to let me help you, okay?"

Ellen let out the biggest breath and hugged her daughter tightly.

"Okay, my darling, okay."

Chapter 9

The rest of the week carried on pretty much the same. Thea would get up, go see Ryder, then train with Jolene. Her afternoons were for cramming in as much Witch law as she could with Margret and learning about her new world with Simon.

Ryder was almost back to his old self now; Thea was steadily seeing an improvement in him each day.

Turning the corner and arriving at her boyfriend's door this morning, something wasn't right. She could hear muffled moaning coming from his room. She crept up to the door to listen; fear quickly settled in, fear that someone was in there torturing him all over again. She couldn't take it any more. She forced the door open and readied herself for anything. No one was there, just Ryder in his bed, thrashing around in his sleep. The covers were thrown to the floor. He lay on his bed in nothing other than an old pair of grey jogging bottoms. His top half was bare. Beads of sweat glistened all over his body. His hair stuck to his head, and his face was twisted in pain.

Thea watched him for a little bit before going over; she didn't know what to do or how to help him. She had always been told to never wake a sleeping person too quickly; it could cause them harm. She stood watching him nervously. She had her shoes still held in her hand. She hadn't put them on as she wasn't supposed to be going to Ryder's room this early. She was trying to muffle the sound of her footsteps as she crept along the hallways.

Her hair was down today she had gotten up early and straightened it. She had tried to make an effort this morning, wanting to show Ryder she could look pretty when she wanted to. Even though he says she always looks beautiful to him. Instead of her workout clothes, she was in black jeans and a light pink strappy top, her workout clothes were in a bag by the door.

"No, please, not again, I can't take any more," Ryder's voice ripped through the air, making Thea jump. She bent down beside him and reached out her hand to soothe him, but her touch only made him worse.

"Please, please don't, I will do anything you ask, father, please, just not that again," he screamed out. So much pain and anguish coated his voice. Thea wanted to cry, to pull him close to her, hug him and make it all go away.

"Ryder, wake up, you're okay, it's me, Thea," she tried to coax him awake. She couldn't bear to watch him thrash around the bed any longer; hearing him like this was killing her.

He knocked her outstretched hand away from his face.

"Don't touch me. I hate you!" he hissed at her. She knew he wasn't really talking to her and that it was all part of his nightmare, but the words still stung. Her voice shook as she tried again to pull him away from the demons tormenting his dreams. She steeled her nerves, reached over and grabbed him by the shoulders and looked him square in his sweaty trembling face.

"Ryder, you need to wake up now. It's all a bad dream; I'm here for you! I won't ever leave." She paused. He had stopped resisting her, sparking hope that she was reaching him. "Wake up, handsome man, I need you," she whispered delicately in his ear, her eyes were closed. She didn't know what else to do other than shake him, but she didn't want to do that.

"Th…Thea?" his voice croaked out. Her head snapped up.

"You're awake." She didn't know whether to laugh, cry or both. "Are you okay?" she breathed. "You were screaming; it was awful," she rested her forehead on his; she had practically climbed on top of him in the bed.

He took a few deep breaths

"I'm fine. It was just a bad dream." But he knew all too well that it wasn't just a bad dream. "Umm, not that I don't love having you draped all over me, but I need to shower. I stink," he tried to make light of the situation and throw her his normal charming smile, but the light that normally shone in his eyes was not there. Thea could tell it was fake. She wiggled out of the way anyway, allowing him to shuffle off the bed. He stood up, kissed her lightly and turned to leave.

"I'll be right back," he called over to her.

She watched him go but wasn't happy with his nightmare story. She knew it was more.

Less than fifteen minutes had passed when Thea couldn't stand waiting any longer. Ryder had been in his bathroom the whole time. Normally he was in and out like a shot. She was so worried about him; this was so unlike him. Walking over to the bathroom door, she knocked lightly. She could hear the shower was running but nothing else. Her heart pounded; she couldn't believe she was about to walk in on her boyfriend stark naked in the shower. But she couldn't wait any longer; she had to make sure he was okay.

"Ryder? Are you okay in there?" she called through the door. There was no reply, so she went for it and pushed the door open.

Steam billowed out, surrounding her in its warmth. She couldn't see anything. Stepping into the room, she waited for the fog to clear.

"Ryder, I'm sorry, but I'm coming in," she called out, hoping to warn him just in case, so he could at least cover himself up. What she was actually greeted with, though, was not what she was expecting. Ryder was curled up in a ball on the floor in the corner, silently sobbing.

"Oh, Ryder," she rushed over to him and threw herself down next to him. She tugged on his arm until he moved over to her. She wrapped her arms around him and rocked him back and forth, holding his head in her lap. "Tell me what happened. Tell me how I can help?" she spoke to him gently.

He just shook his head but didn't let go.

"That wasn't a bad dream, was it?" she asked him, but still no reply. "Ryder, was that a memory?" she asked.

Sniffing, he slowly pulled himself up until he was sitting. His head was hanging down and he wouldn't meet her gaze.

"My life before was not so perfect. My father was cruel, he would do whatever it took to get what he wanted." he allowed the words to fall from his mouth. "I have spent months learning to overcome a lot of bad memories, feelings and thoughts. But the mind-reading undid all my work like it was nothing," he confided in her. Thea held his hand; it was her turn to trace circles on his hand for a change. "I didn't want you to see that side. I didn't want you to see any of that," he confessed.

"How long have you been having these dreams?" she asked him.

"Every day since the mind reading," he admitted, still refusing to look her in the eye.

"Oh, Ryder, why didn't you say? Why didn't you let me help you?" she asked him, full of concern.

He shrugged. "I'm meant to be the strong one for you; you have so much on your plate right now you don't need this, too," finally he looked up at her. A tear fell down his cheek.

"You idiot," she said and smiled at him. She reached up and clasped her hands around the back of his head. Pressing her forehead to his, forcing him to look nowhere but at her. "I'm here for you just like you are there for me; it's what you do when you lov…" she trailed off, instant heat rose to her cheeks. He couldn't help but grin. she held her eyes tightly closed as the heat engulfed her cheeks and travelled down her neck. He chuckled; she knew just how to cheer him up, and move his mood from bad to good. She kept surprising him every day. No one had ever been able to help him as Thea could. Never had he ever let anyone close enough to him.

"Okay, Princess, thank you. I will take that shower now, okay?" he said.

"Yeah, maybe you should. You do stink, actually," she laughed.

"Oh charming, thanks," he replied, but this time his smile was true. I need to get changed myself, she said as she left the room, the steam in here has done nothing good for me. I'll be back in a little bit, she called as she left the bathroom.

Ryder wasn't ready for his girlfriend to come back so quickly; he'd had a really hard time that morning but was relieved with how it went with Thea. He took longer in the shower than he thought. He was feeling much better, if a little bit embarrassed.

Thea was so quiet when she came in; she caught him singing to himself with his back to her. He wasn't even fully dressed. He sounded amazing; she had never heard him sing before, she didn't know he could.

She tried to stay as quiet as she could; she wanted to hear him sing some more.

"Is there nothing this boy can't do?" she wondered. Ryder

had turned around and caught her staring,

"How long were you standing there?" he asked, but at least he was smiling.

"Long enough to find out how amazing you are," she said with a little laugh.

"I don't sing much any more. I used to sing all the time until it drew too much attention," he told her. She could tell he was trying to act normal like nothing had happened. She was more than happy to let him do that; he didn't need any more mortifying moments today. "There was this club down one of the back streets in town; I used to sing there a lot. The band there needed a singer, so a few nights a week I would step up and sing for them," he said sheepishly.

"I wish I could have seen you," she grinned. "Not that my mum would have ever let me go to a club, though," he stared at her. "How did you get in as you're not much older than me?" she questioned.

"I'm almost nineteen, but I can fool anyone into thinking I'm whatever age I want," he said smugly. "You know what; I know it will be totally reckless and dangerous but do you fancy going there with me? I know the band will be there tonight," he did the most adorable puppy eyes.

"How will we get past the guards and the wards?" she worried.

"Come on, sweetheart, with your awesome amount of power mixed with my not-so-awesome but still pretty epic power, we can get past anything, have faith," he laughed. Thea couldn't help but let a smile slip; how could she even try to resist that face.

Training that morning was boring; Thea couldn't focus on anything other than her night out. She had to keep catching herself, as Jo was able to read her mind. The hall was dull as the sky was grey outside, no sunshine shone through to brighten the place up. Other students tried to sneak into Thea's training sessions to see what all the fuss was about. But Daniel was normally on the case. When he wasn't patrolling the grounds, he would jump in on the training with Jo. Thea dreaded it at first, but now she quite liked having him there. She found him a challenge lately; Jo had been going easy on her. Maybe it was more Jo was getting too tired; the council had her running here, there and everywhere on top of training Thea.

"Thea, I'm fine. Stop thinking I need a break. I'll say if I do, don't worry, I'm tougher than I look," Jo smiled at her.

"Oi, stay out of my head. When are you going to teach me to block that anyway?" she called out.

"When I can fit it in, but it does need to be soon," Jo answered.

"Come on, ladies, less chit chat, more combat," Daniel called out as he came into the room. The room always fell silent when he arrived.

"Has he always been such a stick in the mud?" Thea thought and projected it to Jo. She assumed if she thought what she wanted to say and then thought of Jo, she would know she wanted her to hear it. Jo's face was a picture, pure shock.

"Thea, did you just seriously do that?" Jo thought back.

"Do what?"

"THAT, project your thoughts to me; we are talking through our minds, which normally takes witches ages to learn!" Jo told her.

"Oh, then yeah, I guess I did," Thea tried not to laugh. She had never stunned Jo before, and it felt great.

"My goodness, you really are amazing," Jo thought. Thea did laugh out loud this time. Sweat poured down Thea's back.

She had to call a stop as she found it too funny listening to Jo gush over how amazing she apparently was and seeing Dan's confused face. He had no idea what was going on; it truly was brilliant.

"You're blocking me from your mind already you know," Jo said out loud. "There have been times today when your mind has been totally quiet. I couldn't gauge anything from you," she concluded. Thea was thrilled to hear it.

"Okay, you two, what's going on? You have both been staring at each other for a while now, and Thea is laughing. I don't think you're taking this threat seriously enough," Daniel piped up. Thea huffed.

"Dan, we are taking it seriously; lighten up a little." Daniel puffed up; he wasn't used to anyone; especially a very new younger witch, telling him to lighten up.

"Who exactly do you think you are?" he spat out. "Just because everyone else is fawning all over you doesn't mean I will. People have to earn my respect; it's not just given," he spoke in such a threatening tone.

"Dan, calm down. She didn't mean anything by it," Jo spoke up for Thea, whereas Thea just looked at him. She hadn't responded to him; she just continued to look at him. She could feel this odd tingling starting in her fingers and toes. It didn't take long to spread to the rest of her body.

"No, she was big enough to make the remark; let's see the little girl's reply. Let her stand on her own two feet, shall we? See if she can hold herself against real power!" he declared. Thea still just looked at him. When he raised his arms, ready to call forth his power, that was when Thea made her move.

She had full control of her body, but she had no idea how she was doing it.

"I wouldn't do that if I were you," she said. He didn't listen, he just continued gathering his power. His outstretched hands continued to move around in a circular motion as if he was rubbing a large round object. She could somehow feel how much energy he was controlling; she could see it gathering around his hands. He had no intention of backing down. Thea had disrespected him in front of others, and he wasn't going to let it slide. Thea heard a tiny voice within her mind.

"Take the power from his control, stop him before he even has a chance to use it," the voice spoke to her.

"How?" she asked back, somehow. She knew she was speaking with the element Air.

"He wields a small amount of my power, whereas you can wield my full power. You already know what to do," Air told her.

Thea brought herself back to the here and now. She looked at Daniel's smug face and sort of pitied him. for what she was about to do was going to knock him down a peg or two, and she was going to do it in front of the small crowd that had begun to form.

Thea lifted her arm and reached her hand out as if to pick something up. She reached with her mind and just plucked the blue ball of energy right out of Daniel's hands. When she opened her hand once more, the tiniest ball of blue light danced on her palm.

The disbelief on his face was priceless. He kept trying to gather more power, but he just couldn't; all the power was in Thea. She had denied him access to it, and she was going to prove her point.

"You may be strong in the element of Air, high councilman, but I'm stronger in every element. I have been granted access to all of the elemental's power, not just the small fraction you are granted. I mean no disrespect towards you whatsoever, and yes, you are right. I have so much to learn still, but please remember I am on your side. I'm not a threat to you," Thea spoke clearly and calmly while holding the small blue ball in her palm.

Daniel was mortified yet awed by Thea. She had taken every ounce of his power in seconds as if it was nothing to her. He couldn't find the words; he didn't know how to respond to what had just happened. Instead, he just turned and quickly walked away, still staring at his hands. The room was silent for a moment before it exploded in noise; everyone spoke at once. Thea released the ball of energy, and it flew back to Daniel. She saw it settle back within him as he looked back over his shoulder at her. He knew she had returned what was his, but he refused to show any gratitude for it.

"Whoa, Jo, I got to leave. I don't want to deal with this, no, I don't fully know how I did it, and no, I can't answer any questions right now," Thea said into Jo's mind before she sprinted out of the room.

Thea spent the rest of the day hiding from everyone, the only person she wanted to see what Ryder. Well, and Jason, but that wasn't going to happen, not right now anyway. Things were just too crazy; it wouldn't be safe for her very human, non-magical friend.

She wandered around until she found a room that looked half abandoned, as if it hadn't seen a living soul in over a decade. Dust covered every surface, as well as the floor. Two of the windows were actually boarded up, and everything had cobwebs on it. She made her way through the dust and the gloom towards the back of the room. She found an old-looking sofa with a tan-coloured throw over it. She pulled the throw off, which was pretty heavy, considering. Underneath was the most beautiful looking sofa she had ever seen; yes it needed a bit of love to bring it up to its full potential, but stunning nonetheless. The cushions looked like they were covered in rich purple velvet, and the legs must have been mahogany. The detail in the woodwork was outstanding.

"Wow, why would they hide such a beautiful thing?" she thought. She plonked herself down on her new favourite piece of furniture. "Ugh, I wish you were here, Ryder; I need you, but I can't come and find you right now," she spoke out loud. She sighed and sank deeper into the comfort of the cushions.

"Bloody hell, Thea, are you talking to me through my mind?" Ryder's voice broke through her thoughts. Thea jumped half a mile into the air, or so it seemed.

"Umm, I guess I am, and no, I don't know where I learnt to do it," she answered him.

"What's wrong? where are you?" he sounded worried.

"I don't really know, I had a bit of a hard time earlier, and I needed to get away from all the people. I just started walking and ended up here," she imagined the room exactly as it was.

Ryder gasped. "You can send images as well? You never fail to surprise me," he told her. "I'll find you; sit tight."

"Thea, wake up," Ryder gently urged her. "It took me longer than I thought to find you, but here I am," he beamed at her. "I never even knew this was up here," he told her.

"Huh; sorry, what?" she felt confused. Ryder chuckled.

"You were asleep when I finally found you; you looked so peaceful, I didn't really want to wake you," he sat down next to her. "So, this place, how did you find it?" he wanted to know. Thea had to think about it for a moment.

"Honestly, I don't really know. I just kind of got pulled this way," she mumbled.

"What's the matter? You seem lost," he asked her. He took

her hand and started the relaxing circular motion she liked so much.

"I'm surprised you haven't heard already," she began; she didn't know how to feel about it.

"Well, I heard something, but I would rather hear the truth from you. It's the only way to know what's really going on," he said gently.

"Oh," she looked at the ground. Thea spent the next twenty minutes bringing Ryder up to date with the events of the day. Once she was finished, she patiently waited for his reply, but he just sat there with his mouth hanging open. Words seemed to be failing him. "Ryder, you're making me nervous; please say something; anything will do," she urged him.

"Um, uh, well, I don't really know what to say," he replied honestly.

"I'm a monster. I knew it," she sobbed and let her head fall into her hands.

"No, Thea, you're not; I didn't mean it like that. I'm just gobsmacked by the things you can do," awe filled the room. He was amazed by his girlfriend. "Never in my life have I even heard of a witch that can wield power like you, well one, but that was hundreds of years ago," he confessed. This didn't make her feel any better.

"Everyone stares at me like I'm a freak," she muttered. "I miss my old life."

"You're not a freak; you're the most amazing person alive," he told her. He tried to pry her fingers away from her face. "You're pretty strong too," he joked as he tried and failed to move her fingers fully from her cheeks. She couldn't help but laugh. "Now come on, I thought we were planning on escaping again tonight, or have you changed your mind?" he poked her playfully.

"Yes, I need some breathing room from this place," she admitted. "Though saying that, I do love this room, do you think we will be able to find it again?" she pondered.

"You will for sure; I have no doubt in my mind that you could do anything if you want to do it," he told her and kissed her hand. "Come on, beautiful, let's go and paint the town red!"

Finding their way back to the main hall wasn't as hard as they thought it would be. The hard part was yet to come. All the exits were covered now. Guards stood at every door, and new wards had been put up all the way around the estate. Safety was of the utmost importance.

Thea and Ryder stood just out of view of the main entrance.

"So, how do we do this?" Thea asked him.

"Well, I was hoping an idea would have come to me on the way, but right now, I'm coming up blank." They watched the comings and goings for a while to see if they could work out any option at all, then it hit Thea.

"Jo and Dan patrol the perimeter most nights," she said. "Jo said they check every single ward and strengthen them if need be. If we wait until they leave, we could sneak out after them," she said triumphantly

"Well, if you could use your hiding spell, of course, I'll help you like I did last time," she reassured him. He just looked at her shaking his head

"You really are brilliant," he beamed and kissed her once more.

"Okay, be ready. They should be coming soon; I'm sure Jo said it was just after supper they would meet and go out together."

The pair waited in silence. Eventually, a couple of figures came around the corner, apparently, in the midst of a heated argument.

"Now's our chance," Ryder whispered. Thea grabbed hold of his hand a little too tightly. They made their way down the steps as quietly as they could. Luckily the two up in front were too busy snapping at each other to notice muffled footsteps behind them. Daniel reached the door first.

"All I am saying, Jolene, is that you could have at least said something, but no, you just stood there gawping with the rest of them," he huffed as he marched through the door.

"Oh, come on, brother, if it was the other way around, you would have done the same and don't deny it," she called him out.

"Granted, she is very powerful, and yes, that is amazing, seeing as none of us knew about her until a couple of weeks ago. But seriously, the attitude on the kid is annoying," he remarked. Jo mock laughed at her brother.

"You're just being silly now," she scoffed.

Ryder pulled Thea along behind him, keeping away just enough to not be noticed but close enough to get through the door without having to touch it. That way, it really would just look like Jo and Dan had left the building.

"Almost there," she whispered into Ryder's Mind, he smiled to himself. He was falling for this girl way too fast, but he no longer cared. He led them all the way to the far wall, out of sight of any prying eyes.

"Okay, we just need to get past this one ward and we are home free," he told her. "I have no idea how to do it, though," he concluded.

"Don't worry, I think I do," she stated.

"Really? How?" he sounded astounded.

"Honestly, I don't know. I just know I can do it," she made him step aside.

She slid her hand slowly across a small section of the wall.

It felt ice cold. She gave one of the thin spider web-like lines of energy a gentle tug; it just unravelled before her eyes.

"Quick, follow me," she grabbed his hand and literally vaulted them over the wall, again having no idea how. Then she replaced the ward to keep the estate safe. "Right, that should do it," she dusted her hands off like she had done some dirty work and beamed at her boyfriend. "Lead the way," she ordered.

Chapter 10

Neon lights flashed everywhere, orange, yellow and green shone out brightly like a beacon for all to see. The night air was cool and crisp, and the stars shone down beautifully.

This part of town was new to Thea. She hadn't known about it until Ryder had shown her. It was easily missed if you didn't know what you were looking for. Ryder walked causally hand in hand with her as he led her down ally after ally, twisting and turning with ease. He knew this place like the back of his hand.

One little ally they took was darker than the rest. Bins were pushed up against the walls, they were overflowing with rubbish. Thea tried not to breathe too deeply; the smell was not the best.

"Watch your step, sweetheart," Ryder pulled Thea out of the way of a suspicious-looking puddle. "I don't think you would want to clean your shoes if you stepped in that," he laughed.

"Where are we?" she asked him.

"This is the entertainment part of the town, well, the part the locals go to anyway, not the touristy part of town," he told her. "I'm just taking you the back-way round, you know to keep us from being seen by too many people. We don't want to use all our energy up on a cloaking spell when we can just walk a different way," he winked at her and carried on.

"It certainly is the back way, all right," she thought to herself.

"I can hear you, you know," he chuckled. "You are so funny at times." He admired her. As of yet, there really wasn't anything he didn't like about her; she just kept getting better to him.

Since connecting with him earlier, when she sent him a message just by thinking it, he could now hear a lot of what she was thinking; if she fully relaxed.

"Well, stay out of my head then, Mr, if you don't like what you hear," she nudged him.

"Ah, here we are." Just up ahead was a club called Trend, or so Ryder said. All Thea could see was a big heavy looking door with a couple of dumpsters on either side. "Trust me; this is the back door. I used to always use it. It takes you backstage, so we can go straight to the band without having the hassle of waiting at the front door."

Thea followed Ryder up the steps to the door and watched as he pulled it open with ease.

"Wasn't that locked?" she asked him

"Yeah," he replied.

She didn't bother asking. She was quickly coming to terms with the fact that her new boyfriend had many ways of going about things, most of them different from hers.

The inside of the club wasn't much better than the outside. It was darker than she thought it would be and very, very loud. Her shoes stuck to the floor as she moved down the corridor, making that horrible squelchy noise as she went.

"Well, I hope it gets better the further in we go," she thought, causing Ryder to laugh.

"I forgot; you are my innocent little princess," he teased her. "Don't worry, I'll protect you from the big bad people."

Thea thought of ways to get him back for teasing her, which only led to him laughing more.

"You really are going to need to learn to shield your mind from me if you want even one of those cute little plans to work," he sang over his shoulder to her.

"Shut up," she huffed at him.

Ryder led her up a couple more steps and around a couple more corners; the volume increased with each step they took.

"Right, in here is where the band gets ready. I'll introduce you if you like," he smiled at her.

She nodded back. She was beginning to feel nervous, and doubted if coming here was really a good choice or not.

"Bloody hell, Ryder, long time no see mate; where have you been?" a male voice boomed out of the door. Ryders's hand was yanked out of Theas as he was pulled into a bear hug.

"Steve, nice to see you mate. I have been busy and what not," he said to the newcomer. "This is Thea," he said as he reached back behind him to grab her hand, pulling her up beside him.

"Oh! I see you have been busy," the new guy joked.

"Nice to meet you Miss. Come on in, the two of you," he beckoned them in. "Excuse the mess; Tom here isn't the tidiest," he said.

"Oi, I heard that," another guy replied. Thea assumed it must be this Tom.

"So, what brings you here, mate? We haven't seen you for what? It must be coming up six months now," he asked.

"Yeah, something like that, and well, I got a free night and thought I would come and see you guys, see if you needed a singer for a few sets," Ryder enquired.

Steve grinned. "We have a permanent singer now, but sure, we can't refuse a talent like yours now, can we?" he said. "Ah, here she is now." Steve pointed at the other side of the room where a door Thea hadn't seen opened.

A tall slim stunning brunette walked towards them. She was making a beeline towards Ryder, all smiles and hip swaying.

"Hi, I'm Stacey, and you are?" she said in a very sultry voice.

"Hey, I'm Ryder, and this is my girlfriend, Thea," he said pointedly. He could feel the anxiety roll off Thea.

Stacey snapped her head round to look her up and down.

"Oh, I didn't see you there, sorry, must have missed you," was all she said, before rolling her eyes and looking back towards Ryder.

"Rude much," Thea thought. Ryder pulled Thea by the hand, so she was closer to him.

"Relax, she's not a patch on you," he said in her mind.

"We go on in five minutes, Stacey. Ryder is going to do a couple of songs with us tonight; he used to sing for us all the time," Steve told her; she was not impressed.

"Steve, we haven't learnt any duets, plus how am I to know if his voice is as good as mine," she huffed. She even stamped her foot a little.

"Stacey, sweetheart, you're brilliant and I love you, you know that, but Ryder will be singing solo," Steve said very gently.

"What?" Stacey wasn't happy at all.

"End of, Stace, so leave it," Steve's word was final.

Stacey glared their way before flicking her hair and sulking off.

"Where do I go when you go and sing? I don't know this place or anyone in it," she asked him, her nerves almost getting the better of her. Ryder sat down on the arm of a very shabby-looking sofa and pulled Thea down with him. She lent up against him.

"Listen, I'm not going to let anything happen to you. I brought you here to show you a good time and to show you one of the things I used to love to do. You can stand at the edge of the stage if you like, that way I'm right near you," he smiled at her and kissed her cheek.

"Okay," was all she said. She didn't want to do anything right now other than stay right where he was. That Stacey girl was throwing her murderous looks; she never seemed to blink; it was weird.

"So, what do you want to sing mate?" Steve asked him.

"I don't mind. You just play, I'll sing along; you know how I am," Ryder told him. All the while, Stacey was still staring at them.

"Ignore her," he whispered to her. "Come on, let's go find you a good spot so you can see everything, yeah?" Ryder dragged Thea up and led her out the door.

Standing at the edge of the stage was different to what she thought it would be; it wasn't very glamorous, really. Not like they made it out to be on TV. There were wires everywhere, lights shining in every direction. People would push past you without even a hint of an excuse me.

Thea hung back by one of the musty old grey curtains. She had poked her head out round the side to see what the main club looked like. She couldn't see too much but what she could make out wasn't really what she had been imagining. The club was situated in an old thirties-style building with a proper old theatre-style stage. The owners had adapted the lighting and speakers to the style of the place, which was actually pretty cool. The dance floor was big from what she could see. There were the odd few tables dotted around the sides and a couple at the back. She could see giant smoke machines on either side of the stage and hundreds of different coloured lights. At the very back and to the left was a box raised quite high up, where she assumed the person controlling all the lights would sit. At the far end of the room was the first of two bars, which right now was teeming with every different kind of person you could imagine. The other, much smaller bar, was on the right side of the room and closer to the stage.

The thing that caught Thea the most though; was the smell of the place; it was a mixture of every different type of perfume and aftershave mingled with sweat. She wasn't a big fan of it.

"You okay, babe?" Ryder appeared behind her and wrapped his arms around her waist.

"Yeah, sure. Hey, you have never called me babe before," she grinned at him, he kissed her one last time.

"Wish me luck," he said as he got ready with his microphone.

Thea settled her nerves and turned to watch Ryder do his thing. She couldn't believe that right now, she was doing something normal teenage girls would be doing. Never did she think she would sneak into a club at any age, let alone underage. She needed this right now; she really needed some normalcy. Yes, it was dangerous, and she knew she was in a whole world of trouble when she got back later, but right now, even though she was a bit scared, she loved it.

The band came past her then, there were four guys in the band, and she hadn't even thought to ask Ryder the band's name. She only knew two of the members' names, well and the singer. As the lights came on and the crowd saw the guys on stage, the whole place erupted in noise. She could hear hundreds of girls screaming, and she couldn't resist a peek around the curtain again.

Everyone had pushed right up to the stage now the guys were ready to play. She could almost see the colour of a few girls' eyes; she quickly whipped her head back round. She didn't want to be seen.

"Hey everyone, we hope you're having a good night tonight!" Steve shouted out to the crowd, causing another belt of screams from the girls and the few odd I love you screeched at him.

"We have a special guest with us tonight, someone we haven't seen for a while, so you guys are in for a real treat," he continued.

"Oh, please say it's the cute guy," Thea heard one girl shout out; she was way too excited right now.

Thea smiled and looked over to the stage entrance. Ryder stood clutching his microphone with a smile on his face; she could tell he was nervous yet buzzing to get back out there.

He turned and winked at her; he blew her a kiss just before stepping onto the stage. The whole place exploded with noise; she wasn't ready for the sheer volume of it. Thea had to step back. She was amazed by the reaction Ryder was getting. She couldn't blame them though, he was gorgeous.

"Oh… my… goodness, they all love him, and he is with me!" the thought made her dizzy.

"Hey everyone," Ryder's voice echoed through the room. "Long time no see," he laughed as the girls screamed louder.

It took a while for them to quieten down before he could say anything else.

"So, I'm going to sing a few songs with the guys here for you all tonight. I hope that is okay?" he asked, knowing all too well the girls would just scream the place down again. He was enjoying it way too much.

"Okay, let's do this," he shouted over his shoulder. The music started up, and Thea was just as excited to watch Ryder as the rest of the girls in the club. When he opened his mouth and his voice sang out, she was practically knocked backwards. He was a million times better than he was when she caught him that morning.

He stole a look her way and tried not to laugh when he caught sight of her shocked face.

"Ha-ha Thea your face is brilliant, better than you thought huh," he spoke into her mind.

"I have no words," was all she could say back.

When the song ended the place shook with screams. Thea felt someone behind her. She looked up to see Stacey inches away. All ready to go on after Ryder.

"Hmm, not bad I guess," she huffed. Thea really didn't like this girl but she kept her mouth shut.

"He's cute, though. How exactly did you get him?" she insulted Thea.

Thea just looked at her; she couldn't believe someone would be so blunt to her face. Before she could answer though, Ryder was talking again.

"This next song is something I have just written, and it's for someone very special to me," he declared.

Some girl in the audience shouted that she would be his girlfriend, which he heard and he had to laugh.

"Sorry, sweetheart, that position is already filled," he answered; this was followed by a chorus of no's and a load of upset girls.

"But yes, this song is for my girlfriend, who is here tonight," he shouted out.

Thea was totally shocked; never had she ever had anyone do anything like this for her.

"Aren't we the lucky one," came Stacey's snide remark.

Thea took a deep breath. "Yes, I am, aren't I?" she replied, and gave her a fake smile before pointedly turning her back to her.

Thea looked out across the crowd; something felt off. It wasn't just the fact she was outside her comfort zone. It was more than that. It was as if she could feel something in the air. She continued to scour the place for anything unusual. She knew she was using magic of some kind because she had begun to feel everyone's emotions, which she hadn't been doing before.

Behind her was a strong feeling of jealousy, she knew that was just Stacey; she ignored her. She sent her senses further out across the room.

"This is so odd; how am I doing this?"

She felt normal things like happiness, excitement, tiredness even a bit of fear, but mostly people were giving off a messed up drunk feeling. She shook it off. Putting it down to being in a very overcrowded room and being so new to her powers, it was probably a power sensory overload.

Ryder was coming to the end of his song at this point and was pointing and waving to the girls in the audience. He kept looking over at Thea, though and winking.

There it was again, that horribly wrong feeling. She hadn't imagined it this time. Ryder must have felt something too. His whole energy changed at the same time; he looked right at Thea and knew she felt it too.

"Stay where you are, don't move. I'll finish here and come straight to you; something isn't right," he spoke in her mind.

Thea didn't dare move, for Ryder to worry meant something must be up. She was slowly filling with fear; all she wanted to do was run.

"Okay, that's me done for tonight guys. It has been a pleasure as always; hopefully, see you all soon," Ryder bid the crowd farewell and walked off towards Thea, ignoring all the sad shouts and cries from the many, many girls in the room.

"You okay?" he asked her. Once he had hold of her, he felt better, more in control of the situation. "Did you feel that too, Yeah?" he asked.

"Yes, what is it?" she answered.

"I don't know, but there is a threat here. I don't know where or how bad, but we have to go," he told her.

"Could it just be Stacey? She clearly hates me," Thea tried to joke but knew now wasn't the time. Ryder ignored her last statement and grabbed her hand.

"Come on, we better go now," he dragged her along behind him. They retraced their steps back to the door they had come through earlier. "I think it's best if we use the cloaking spell. I can't risk them getting too close to you," he whispered to her.

"Who are they? Do you know?" she was officially scared.

"No, I don't know yet, but hopefully, we will soon," he said.

Ryder tried to listen at the door before pulling it open. He muttered the words to the cloaking spell just before stepping out. Thea channelled her power through her hands and into him to help steady the spell; they both needed to be hidden, not just her.

"Let's go. Only speak with your thoughts, don't risk it any other way," he instructed her.

"I'm scared," was all she replied.

"I'm here. I won't ever let anyone hurt you."

That was when they saw three rather big guys step around the corner from them, followed by two slightly older women.

"I'm sure I felt them, this way, ma'ams," one of the guys said to the women behind them.

"They're quite young. They can't hide from us forever," another one added.

"Less chatting, more searching," one of the women snapped

back.

"I want that child before those other idiots get their hands on her. She is just what the Willows need. If we could get her, we would get her mother back too," the other woman said. Thea froze.

It was the Willow witches.

Chapter 11

"Breathe, just breathe and don't make a sound," Thea coached herself.

Ryder held her hand, and he wasn't moving a muscle. It felt as if all the air had been sucked out of Thea's lungs. She felt as if she was going to pass out.

"Come on, surely they couldn't have gone far; they're just kids, for Pete's sake," one of the women said.

"Audrey, remember who the girl's mother is," the other woman reminded her.

"The day she slipped out of our grasp is not one I will soon forget, Janet; you don't need to remind me," the other woman snapped back.

"If we find her kid and lure her out, maybe all will be forgiven!" the one called Audrey said, the blood drained from Thea's face.

"Don't panic; I promised you I would protect you, and I will," Ryder told her. He sounded like he would kill anyone that tried to hurt her.

"They are after my mum. What do I do?" she worried

"Don't get caught. That is what we do. Just wait until they move around the corner, then we can move out in the opposite direction," he instructed her.

"The whole bloody town is crawling with Nightshade members. We only have this one real chance; don't mess it up," Janet ordered the three guys escorting them.

"Did you hear that?" Ryder asked her. "We need to move now. It's worse than I thought; if they catch us, it's bad enough, but the Nightshades, they're much worse," he admitted.

Thea and Ryder inched their way along the steps, hardly breathing, watching every move they made, trying not to draw attention to their hiding place.

"That's it, keep going, go down to the left and keep moving."

They made it to the end of the ally without detection. Thea allowed herself to look back over her shoulder; what a big mistake. She had forgotten about the disgusting puddle she had avoided a few hours before. If the noise of her foot splashing down didn't draw their attention, then the ewe sound she let slip was a sure give away.

"Over there, I heard something. Quickly, you idiots, quickly," Audrey shouted at her group.

"Thea, we need to run; they know we are here now. This spell won't hide us for long," Ryder's voice was urgent. "Move," he literally dragged her behind him. Forgetting her legs were nowhere near as long as his, she couldn't keep up.

All pretence at being stealthy was forgotten. They ran as fast as they could out of the winding back allies.

"Please don't let go," Thea begged him. "I don't know the way."

Ryder's face settled into a steely resolve; he meant business now. He promised he would look after her, and that is what he intended to do.

It wasn't long before they came bursting out of the back streets into the main street.

"Okay, we need to get home without delay. We can't afford to mess up," he told her

"I'm sorry, Ryder, I really am. I didn't mean to step in the puddle," she apologised.

"Don't worry, let's go," he urged her on. She had never seen him so serious before; he was scarily beautiful. They walked in silence for a while, both too scared to make a sound just in case they were overheard.

They were both exhausted by the time they reached the street the Brockmoor estate was on. They had only just managed to shake the Willow members off their tails minutes ago.

Thea had somehow increased her power flow, muting all ways of sensing their power for a short amount of time. When their trail went cold, the Willow members finally gave up.

Thea was shaking; the spell took a lot from her. She had drawn power from her earth elemental friend, but even though she had help, it wasn't easy for her to do. She was just too new to all of this.

"Thea, will you be able to open the wards again to get us back through, or are we going to have to do this the hard way and use the front gate?" Ryder dreaded her answer because he already knew what it would be.

Thea looked up at the wall and lifted her trembling hand. She tried to focus on the energy flow of the wards, but it was no good, everything was throbbing, and nothing would stay still.

"I'm sorry, I don't think..." she tried to say before she tumbled to the floor. Ryder only just caught her in time.

"Thea!"

There was nothing for it; he wasn't going to let his pride get the better of him. He scooped her up as gently as he could and made his way around the front of the building. As his foot crossed the threshold, all kinds of alarms were set off. Guards came rushing out from all angles. Ryder did the only thing he could and just stood stock still. His world was about to get a whole lot harder.

The Brockmoor estate's courtyard was full of Witches within seconds. Thea's mum came rushing out of the main door, and she pushed her way through the gathering crowd.

"THEA!" Ellen's voice rang out loudly. "What happened? What is wrong with her?" she was shaking.

"I think she is just exhausted; she used quite a bit of power tonight," Ryder hesitantly said, still clutching her to his chest.

"YOU!" Ellen shouted and pointed at Ryder. "Every time something happens to my daughter, she is with you," Ellen accused him.

"Ms Jameson, I swear it's not like that. You know I would never let Thea get hurt; I would do anything for her," he tried to make her understand.

"You have got a lot of explaining to do, young man," Margret's voice boomed out across the courtyard. She was stood at the main door.

"Let him through," she demanded. "You two take her to the infirmary, quickly," she pointed at two young men.

Ellen went with them, of course.

"Ryder, follow me, please," she turned away and left through the door she had appeared. Knowing he would follow.

Ryder could feel every eye on him. The corridor was practically lined wall to wall with people gawping at him. He felt so uncomfortable. He held his head high, though; he wasn't going to give these judgemental people the satisfaction of making him feel he was to blame for all of this. The girls that were infatuated with him only days before stood staring smugly at him as he passed.

Margret was already seated when he entered her room. He pulled out a chair opposite her and sat down; he didn't wait for an invitation.

"Explain," was all she said.

He sighed. "Is there really any point? None of you will believe me anyway," he said sadly. "Ever since you found out about my past, you have judged me," he finished.

"Now listen here, young man, we took you in when you said you had no one and had lost yourself," she spoke clearly but sternly. "Yet you turn around and disrespect us by lying and hiding who you are. How can you blame us for how we act now?" she asked him.

He knew she had a point, but he hadn't hidden anything from them other than that. He let them invade his mind, and that weakened him for weeks. He had agreed to an escort for the majority of the day as well. What more could he do to please these people?

"Look, I swear I didn't do anything to her. We were talking about things we liked to do and how much she wanted a break. All the stress you lot have thrown at her in such a small space of time was dragging her down," he paused. "Oh, don't look at me like that, ma'am, you know it to be true. Yes, she needs to catch up, but damn, you lot push her to the extreme; it's like you only see what you can gain from her, not who she actually is," he accused her. "She is a person first, the magic is just part of who she is. It's not the only thing that defines her, and she shouldn't have to feel like something you own," he was getting angry.

Margret's face was a picture. She was rapidly losing her calmness as well.

"All you council members are the same. You're all so worried that if you don't secure her for your own, a different coven will, and they will be better, stronger, and more powerful than you. It doesn't matter which coven you're from; you're all the same. And yes, I am comparing you to the Nightshades and the Willows. You may believe you're better than the others, ma'am, but when it comes to human decency, kindness and compassion, all of you are seriously lacking. Maybe you should strive for that instead of being revered as the best," he finished saying, his heart was pounding, and his stomach was in his mouth.

He couldn't quite believe he had let all of that spill out at once. It's one thing to think it, but to actually say it was another. He was shaking, but he was oddly proud of himself.

"Well, are you quite done?" Margret seethed at him. He held her gaze.

"I was more than prepared to tell you what had happened tonight, but if I'm honest, I think it's best to wait for Thea. She will explain to you as you won't bother believing me even if I did; all I will say is the town is riddled with not only Nightshade members but Willow members too. However you plan to keep Thea safe, it better include her mother as well, as she is of interest to them too," he snapped at her.

"Right, I'm guessing we are done here for now then. Mark my words, once that girl is awake, the two of you will be explaining everything in detail, and there will be no backing out of it," she warned him. "Now leave," she ordered Ryder out of her office.

Ryder stood and left. He wasn't going to give her the satisfaction; she wouldn't see how very mad he truly was. All he wanted to do now was go back to his room and stay there until Thea was back up and about. He didn't get far, though, when Daniel cornered him.

"You're coming with me," Daniel growled. He grabbed Ryder by the elbow and guided him down the hallway to an abandoned room. Two other men he didn't know were sitting waiting in there. Daniel shut the door behind him.

"Sit down," Daniel told him.

"Oh great," Ryder thought. "Look, fellas, I am not going to fight you," Ryder said.

Daniel laughed. "I'm not here to fight you, you stupid boy, the other council members won't do what needs to be done, but I will. If you don't tell us everything we need to know about the Nightshades and their plans, then we will just have to personally hand-deliver you back to them," Daniel told him; his smile had a vile tint to it.

"What?" Ryder spat. "I'm not old enough, you don't get included in anything important until your twentieth birthday, and with that, it's the bare minimum; only the ascended truly know it all," he stammered. "I can tell you about the living arrangements and their schooling, but that's about it," he added.

Daniel stared him down. "You sure you don't want to think a little harder about that?" he prodded him.

"Look in my bloody head again if you really want to. There is nothing else there you haven't already ripped out of me." He started to panic. He couldn't go back there; it took everything he had to escape that place the first time around; he would never make it out again if they took him back now. "I know nothing, I swear," he pleaded.

"Sorry, little boy, that's just not good enough," Daniel said, and he heaved Ryder to his feet, "Time to leave."

Hours had passed since Thea had blacked out. She lay sound asleep on one of the infirmary beds. Not the most comfortable things to sleep on but a bed nonetheless. Her mum was right beside her, refusing to leave her side. She was determined to never let her out of her sight again.

The infirmary was a dreary-looking place. All grey and boring. It smelled of bleach and toilet cleaner. All the beds were lined up against one wall, with pristine matching white bedding and white curtain dividers to separate the beds into separate cubicles. Ellen was draped over a high-backed chair. Right next to Thea's head, she held her hand in hopes it would encourage her daughter to wake up.

"Please wake up, my darling. I'm sorry these past few weeks have been so hard on you, so confusing, but I promise I'll make it all better if you just wake up," she begged her daughter's sleeping form. She didn't even move. Ellen sobbed; she held Thea's hand still and just resolved to wait it out.

Thea's hand grew hot, then cold, then hot again.

"What's going on?" her mum muttered. She dropped Thea's hand and stood up; she was going to get the nurse.

"Ryder," Thea murmured. She started to toss and turn on the bed.

"Don't worry, sweetheart, I'm here with you. You don't need to worry about him any more," Ellen stroked her head and tried to soothe her daughter.

"No, I need him," she slowly woke up. "Mum, where am I? Actually, no, just get me to Ryder," she was beginning to sound urgent.

"No, Thea, you are staying right here. You were passed out when we found you, and low and behold, you were in that boy's arms," she told her. "Every time bad things happen to you, you are with him. I know I said I approved of him, but the more I learn, the less I like him. You won't be spending any more time with that boy," her mother told her sternly.

"No, you can't do that. You can't stop me," Thea said

angrily.

"Actually, sweetheart, I can. Until you are eighteen, you will do as I say, seeing as you are only seventeen, you are still under my protection, and I say you can't see that boy any more," her mum wouldn't budge

"No, Mum. Don't do this," she pleaded.

"Thea, my word is final," Ellen had laid the law down, and she wasn't prepared to change it.

Thea rolled over and refused to look at her mum, and silent tears rolled down her face in two endless streams. Thea felt her elements stir within her. She knew they were there. Whenever she could feel them strongly, it normally meant something was up; something was going to happen. She took comfort knowing they were with her.

She spent the rest of the night pretending to sleep when in fact, she was trying to think of ways to get to Ryder. She wasn't prepared to lose him, not when she had only just found him. Her mum infuriated her at times.

She had so much she needed to talk about with her, not only about the Willow coven members that were after her but also normal teenage girl things, too. She had no one here other than her mum and Ryder. She didn't know who to trust any more. Everyone seems to want something from her all the time. When all she wanted was a friend to talk to, this was all so new to her still; yes, she knew she was learning very quickly, but that was only due to the elemental help she was magically receiving. She wasn't stupid; she knew everyone was either jealous of her for one reason or another, or they hated her. At the very most, a select few found her fascinating; hence why they were so nice to her. She missed Jason.

"What I would give to see that goofy face of yours. I miss

you so much," she cried to herself.

The sun was starting to creep its way up into the sky when Thea finally allowed herself to drop off into an uneasy sleep. At some point in the early hours, she heard her mum get up and move about. She refused to open her eyes, though, she wasn't ready to talk to her right now; she was still too raw, thanks to her mum's harsh rules. She felt a soft kiss placed upon her head before her mum whispered in her ear

"I'll be back in a little while." She listened to the sound of her footsteps fade away before opening her eyes. She wasn't in the right kind of mood to socialise with anyone, let alone her mum.

She swung her legs off the bed; she was weaker than she realised. Sitting there for a while, she took in the room; she saw her reflection in the mirror on the wall.

"Oh wow, what a state! You look awful!" she reprimanded herself. She wanted to get out of there as soon as possible, but walking was proving very difficult. She didn't dare try to pull any power her way to help her along. So, the slow way it was.

She made it to the door.

"Thea Jameson, I'm sorry, but you cannot leave until the high council lady Grace has said so. I am here to make sure you stay put," a very serious-looking man that was put on guard duty told her.

"Oh, for goodness sake."

Chapter 12

The clock in the infirmary was the slowest yet the loudest clock Thea had ever sat and watched. The hands barely moved. She was convinced they moved backwards. The constant tick, tick, tick was slowly driving her insane.

The nurse that ran the infirmary, her name was Melanie, wouldn't stop fussing around her. Come the end, she had to tell her to back off. She was losing her patience with all this waiting. Margret barged through the doors, causing them to swing inwards and smack into the walls.

"That will be all, Melanie; I'll take it from here," barked Margret.

"I was told to wait here for Grace, not you!" Thea didn't intend to sound so rude, but she just didn't have the time for Margret's antics today. Margret just stared at Thea; you could see she wanted to explode at her but held her tongue.

"She is held up with something, so you get me."

"Lucky me," Thea said sarcastically. She earnt a death glare from Margret.

"Right, let's get this over with, shall we?" the older woman said. "Where did you go last night, and why exactly did you think it would be a good idea to go in the first place?" she stated.

"I.,." Margret didn't give Thea a chance to answer the first question before firing more at her.

"Did it not cross your mind how much danger you were putting the Coven in. How everything we are working for would have been at risk?" she took a breath. "Do you not understand how much everyone is giving up to drag you up to speed on everything, so that you can be a useful functioning member of our Coven?" Margret showed no sign of stopping. "Of course you didn't; you only thought about what you could do to cause as much hassle as you possibly could."

Thea could feel the anger building in her belly. The heat was rising from the very pit of her soul. She couldn't stand this woman. She was only ever interested in what she could gain. She enjoyed bossing people around a bit too much. Thea's hair lifted; she could physically feel her hair go static. Her hands tingled and her head felt very hot.

"Attention-grabbing little miss, that is what you are," Margret continued. Thea had tuned out the bulk of what she had said.

"STOP!" shouted Thea. "You are always going on about listening and learning your place. You always say how I should respect my elders, but clearly you missed the respect lesson," she pointed out. "Have you ever stopped to think how I feel in this? How I am as a person and how this whole situation makes me feel?" she glared at her. "Did it not cross your mind that all the lectures and preparing as you call it, might just be a bit much for someone who is totally new to your world?"

Thea was almost shouting now; Margret was totally taken aback.

"Did you not even for a second think that I might be scared and lonely? I have been thrown into a world I do not know. I lost my home, my friends and everything I had ever known; all for what? So I could be your new pet project? To train so I can be some special secret weapon for you? No, you didn't, did you? Because it isn't happening to you!" Margret's face was stunned.

"I wanted a teenage night, a few hours where all this craziness didn't exist. Ryder is the only person here who tells me the truth, who cares about how I feel, and not just about what he can gain from me! So yes, we went out, and yes, it was great. No, we didn't do it to hurt you, believe it or not, we just wanted to have some fun," she finished. "Are you happy now?" she pointed the question at the older woman.

"Well, I... I'm sorry you feel that way, Thea; that was never our intention. But we do need to know where you went and if you were seen," she carried on saying in a much softer voice

"Oh, my goodness, you really don't care about people at all, do you?" Thea got up and started walking towards the door. "I'm done with your questions; I'm going to find my boyfriend and my mother; we have a few things to discuss. If you have a problem with this, then tough. I'll talk to Grace when I'm ready too, but not you," she said flatly. "And just because I'm a nice person, I will tell you this. No, we weren't seen, but you better get ready as both the Willows and the Nightshades are out there in force," the door shut with quite a bang.

Thea took a few deep breaths; she couldn't believe how she got through that without releasing all the pent-up anger and energy she knew she had building; she could feel it behind her eyes. She felt quite proud of herself for that.

She walked as quickly as she could, she had one destination in mind, and that was to find Ryder. She needed to see him; she had to make sure he was all right and to find out what actually had happened; but mostly she just wanted a hug. She felt like she hadn't seen him for days, and she missed him. Avoiding everyone, she kept her head down and walked straight to Ryder's room, but when she got there it was empty. She was so disappointed, all she wanted was him right then, she didn't know where else to look, he was always here or with her.

Thea went into Ryder's room and sat down on his bed, "I'll just wait here for him," she told herself. She lay down on the bed and sank into the cosiness of his duvet, it smelt like him, and she loved that smell. She couldn't believe how lucky she was, all the girls here wanted him, yet she was the one he chose; but she really didn't know why. She had been lost in thought for a while before she drifted back off to sleep. The amount of power she had used must have zapped her energy worse than she had thought.

"Thea, wake up," her name was being called from far away. She didn't want to wake up; she was having a really good dream. The voice was pretty insistent, though. Slowly she opened her eyes.

"Ryder?" she uttered his name, but it wasn't him shaking her.

"Thea! Are you okay, darling?" Ellen worried.

Thea's heart sank. It was her mum.

"Mum, what are you doing here?" Ellen sat down next to her.

"I have been looking for you everywhere, I went back to the infirmary and you weren't there, I checked our rooms too, and you weren't there either, so I guessed you would be here!" she smiled. Thea sat up.

"I'm fine! See?" she was still angry with her mum.

"Look, darling, I know you are mad right now, but I'm only doing this because I love you. I can't see you get hurt again; I wouldn't be able to bare it if anything happened to you," she tried to explain to her daughter.

Thea was having none of it, though.

"Ryder isn't an issue Mum, I wanted to go out last night. He just came with me; in fact, it was him that kept me safe," she told her. "I get that I have all this power that everyone is very keen to help me learn to harness, but right now, it's all a bit much. I want

144

to be allowed to learn at my speed and to spend time with my boyfriend. Please try to understand," she urged her mum. She was close to tears.

"Thea, I wish it was that simple, and I wish it were up to me, but it's not," she spoke softly." I wish I could let you just be you, but bigger things are at risk here. You are at risk, and I know that is my fault, I'm sorry, but right now I need to make sure you are prepared," she told her. "Once this is all over, if you still feel the same way, you can pursue it then, but not now. I'm sorry, my love," she said.

"But you said you liked him?" Thea cried at her mum.

"I did! when he wasn't putting your life at risk."

"I got to go. I can't listen to any more of this," she whispered and got up. She didn't look back; she just moved towards the door.

"Where are you going?" her mum called. "Don't you walk away from me, young lady. You are just going to have to accept how things are and get on with it. I'm sorry, I am, but that is the way it is," her mum called after her.

She lifted her hand and waved it forcefully to the right, and Ryder's bedroom door slammed in her mother's face. Thea's feet took her on a path she barely knew; it was as if they had a mind of their own. It wasn't long until she found herself in her little secret room with the comfy sofa once more.

Relieved at last to be on her own, she sank down into the sofa. The tears flowed freely, and she didn't try to stop them. She looked around her new space once more. The whole place was covered in dust sheets. The only thing that wasn't covered was her sofa.

"Hmm, weird," she got up and started to pull the covers off everything. There were beautiful paintings hung on the walls and gorgeous ornate tables, cabinets and bookcases dotted around the room.

"Wow! this is amazing," she turned around and around, taking it all in, the walls were a deep maroon colour with beautiful gold trim. Old wooden beams were spaced evenly across the ceiling. It was a stunning room.

"It's all for you," a voice spoke inside her head; it was the fire element again. Thea jumped.

"Whoa, you got to stop doing that. At least give me some warning," she uttered. "What do you mean it's all for me?" The voice took a while to reply

"You are Isamcey," it said

"Sorry? I'm what?" she was very confused.

"Isamcey, the gifted, the chosen, there are many names, but the ancient ones call you Isamcey," it was taking her a while to let all this new information sink in.

"So, you're telling me I'm something more than I already am? I don't believe you; I can't believe you," she was bewildered.

"The room wouldn't have allowed you entry if you weren't the true Isamcey," she was informed.

"What does this mean for me? What do I have to do?" she asked out loud.

"Right now, nothing, but when the time comes, you will be called upon. It is your right, your destiny," she was told.

"I need Ryder; this is too much," she felt as if she couldn't breathe. She clutched her sides and tried to take deep breaths, and she was beginning to panic.

"Isamcey, the one you seek is not here," she heard the voice say.

"What do you mean! He's not here?" she continued to panic.

"The answers you seek are with the one you admire but do not trust," the fire element told her.

"Stop with all the cryptic rubbish and tell me straight for once," frustration laced her voice.

Her ears popped sharply, and everything was strangely loud. She looked around the room, the elements had left her for now, and she knew it was pointless calling out to them; she wouldn't get an answer.

"The one I admire but do not trust? Who the heck do they mean?" she really racked her brain; right now, she didn't like anyone let alone admire them. Pain raced through her heart; she couldn't believe Ryder would just up and leave without telling her.

"Maybe I was wrong after all; maybe he didn't feel the same way about me."

The training hall was pretty empty when she walked in. Jo was training by herself in the far corner. Thea took a deep breath; she had changed into her workout clothes and tied her unruly hair back into a high ponytail. She walked over and coughed loudly. Jo spun round, startled.

"Oh, Thea, you made me jump." she relaxed. "How do you feel? I hear you had quite a bit of an adventure these past couple of days?" Thea didn't know what to say, she liked Jo, but she didn't trust her. Then it hit her maybe the answers were with Jo.

"Uh, yeah, it was a bit eventful," she forced a smile. "Um, Jo, I need to ask you a few things," she said hesitantly.

"Thea, you can ask me anything, you know that," she reassured her. "What is wrong?" she urged her on.

"Firstly, where has Ryder gone?" she quickly asked. She didn't want to chicken out.

"What do you mean, he's normally where ever you are?" Jo was confused. "Come to think about it, I haven't seen him since he carried you over the estate's threshold," she pondered. Dread settled in Thea's belly. "It's okay, I'm sure he's just hiding away somewhere. He used to like to take himself off sometimes when he first came to us," she reassured Thea. "Was there anything else?" Thea wasn't sure she was ready to ask the next question. She didn't want to sound crazy. "Thea, it's okay, you can trust me, I promise," she gently encouraged her.

That's the problem, though; she didn't trust anyone any more.

"I have been learning a lot since I arrived here, and I just wondered if you could clear a few things up for me?" she proceeded with caution.

"Okay, I'll do my best." Jo was nothing but reassuring, she had always been nice to Thea, but that didn't change the fact she didn't fully trust her.

"Like I said, I have been hearing a lot of different stuff in a short time, and well, I heard something about a thing called Isamcey?" she stopped. Jo's face had subtly changed.

"Where did you hear that? It's not something we talk about any more," her voice shook a bit.

"I can't remember. I just didn't fully understand it and wanted to know what it was," she tried to sound like it wasn't a big deal. Jo was hesitant to speak, but she eventually decided it wouldn't hurt to clue Thea in on the subject.

"Well, Isamcey is a person, not a thing. It's a name given to a person who is gifted with immense power." She told Thea, who was listening very carefully.

"Oh, okay, I see, so how do you become Isamcey?" she asked.

"You don't become Isamcey Thea; you are born Isamcey. I don't mean you are born and named Isamcey. I mean, it's a bit like a destiny, if you are meant to be the Isamcey you will be," she finished.

"How come it's not talked about any more?" Thea was trying to hide her interest.

"Just over a hundred years ago, there was an influx of people claiming to be Isamcey, they stole power from others to try and prove they were the chosen one, and in doing so they started a war and caused a massacre, thousands of good Witches were killed that day, it didn't end well. So, it had been banned since then to teach anything about the Isamcey," she concluded.

"Oh," Thea didn't know what to say. She now had a heavy burden to carry.

"Thea, where did you hear about that? I know you said you don't remember, but I really do need to know," Jo sounded urgent.

"I'm sorry I don't remember," Thea started to walk away. "Thanks though, Jo, see you later," she called.

Thoughts ran through her head, things were getting stranger by the minute. She rounded the corner to see Daniel whispering to a couple of men she hadn't seen before. She couldn't quite make out what he was saying, but it didn't look good. He was acting so shifty.

"Did you get it done? Is he gone?" Daniel asked the other two guys.

"Yes, Sir, the boy is back where he came from," they confirmed.

"What did they say about payment," he asked, but the two guys were getting anxious. "Well, spit it out," he snapped.

"Sir, they said they would not pay for the return of a traitor, but they let us go, and that was our payment," one of the guys said.

"Bloody idiots, he should have been worth a lot. I should have gone myself," Daniel was not happy.

Thea threw her hand over her mouth to stop herself from being heard. She had an awful feeling they were talking about Ryder.

"It won't be long until people realise he's missing. What am I going to say if I have nothing to show for it?" he argued.

"What will they do to him, Sir? Just wondered, that's all; he is just a kid, not even nineteen yet," one of the guys said. Daniel shot daggers at him.

"I don't care, Mick, what they do to him. He's Nightshade scum and needed to go back where he came from, not taint our coven. They can kill him for all I care."

Thea wanted to cry, scream, charge at him, anything, but she knew she couldn't; it was just too dangerous. All she could do was turn and run. She ran to the only person she knew, her mum. She didn't stop until she reached their rooms.

Her mum was sitting quietly in the chair in the corner of the room, and she had been crying. She jumped when Thea barged into the room.

"Thea, what is the matter?" she stood up and went to her daughter.

"It's Ryder. Dan handed him over to the Nightshade coven," she sobbed. "Mum, what do we do?" Thea's mum was silent. "Mum, please?" she was desperate.

"There is nothing we can do. Once they have him, that's it; we won't get him back. I'm so sorry, darling, I truly am."

Thea shook her head violently. "NO, there must be something we can do," she screamed. "Dan hates the Nightshade members, mum. If he finds out, then you will be next," she pointed out. Ellen went pale. "And to make it worse, when we were out, we hid from a group of Willow witches. They aren't after me; they want you. They don't know about my power yet; they just want me to lure you out!" she stated

"We are in big trouble, and I don't think we are in the right place, not any more."

Chapter 13

Ellen sat in silence. Watching her daughter get so upset over a boy she only just met reminded her of herself at Thea's age. She was exactly the same when it came to Aren, she loved him instantly, and she thought he felt the same; she was so sure.

Now her life was so different. Seeing the guy she once loved again would mean awful things for her daughter, and she wasn't prepared for that. Add the Willow witches on top, and she was in a whole world of trouble. If either of them got their hands on her it would turn out badly for Thea, but it would be worse if they got Thea herself. She didn't know what to do.

She loved her daughter and wanted to do anything she could to make her happy, but she wasn't prepared to put her in the direct sight of either of the other two covens. She thought about packing the two of them up and running again, but where would they go. Thea needed more magic training and she couldn't provide that. If she did, it would draw the enemy right to them. But if she stayed here with people who wanted to use Thea for their own benefit, well, Thea would never forgive her.

"Mum," Thea's voice floated in from the bathroom. "I need to tell you something, and you must promise to not freak out!" she told her already nervous mother.

"The elements told me that I am more than I thought I was," she started, she was trying for casual, "They said I'm something called Isamcey," she ploughed on without letting her mother get a world in edgeways. "I found a room that no one else knows about; they say it was meant for me," she rushed to get all the words out. "Mum?" Thea stuck her head around the door. Her mum's mouth was hanging open, and she was shaking. "Mum, say something. What does this mean for me?" she pleaded.

"It… it means we have to go on a bit of a journey," her mum stammered. "The lady I told you about, the one who helped me deliver you. We need to go to her," her mum said. "She will know what to do."

"How will we get there?"

Ellen looked at her daughter, "You're going to need to show me this special room. I can't go there without your permission; trust me, there are a lot of rules!"

Getting to the room was the first challenge. They had to avoid everyone, and that was always hard, as everyone wanted to know what was going on with the new super magic girl. Thea hated it.

They left together, taking nothing with them. Thea led the way.

Ellen was so nervous she was convinced they would get caught. She was surprised by how calm Thea was.

"It's not far now, Mum; just up that flight of stairs and around the corner. It was all going a little bit too well.

Thea stuck close to her mother. It was truly uncanny how much alike the two of them were. When they were stood next to each other, they looked like twins. They had the same colour and length of hair, their eyes were exactly the same, and they even walked the same. The only thing that was different was their choice of clothes. Thea favoured Jeans, old trainers and goofy t-shirts with old cartoon characters on, whereas her mum had cropped three quarter length slacks on with a flowery purple blouse with no sleeves. Both had the same determined look on their faces, though.

"Ah, just who I was looking for," Daniel appeared out of nowhere. "Thea, our little prodigy, Grace has been expecting you. Why don't you run along now? That's a good girl," he sneered at her.

"I'm busy," she replied. He didn't like her tone; it was written all over his face.

"No one is too busy for Grace," he said through gritted teeth. "Ellen, I think we need to have a little chat. Why don't you come with me?" he tried to steer her mother in the opposite direction.

"I said we are busy, Dan. I will see Grace later." Thea stepped towards him, but he refused to budge. "Take your hand off of my mother," she growled.

"I can't do that; we need to have a friendly chat," Daniel was acting tough, but he was sweating; he feared Thea and she knew it. His dark hair was sticking to his face.

Thea was growing angry. She reached out her hand towards her mother; she wasn't going to let her mother be taken by the same slimy snake that had taken her boyfriend.

"It's okay, darling. You go ahead, and I'll meet you later. I promise it's okay," Ellen had to protect her baby. She had to get her out of here, and this was the only way she could see that happening. A single tear slid down her right cheek. Thea saw it and knew what her mum was doing.

"Mum, no," she whispered.

"I loved you then, I love you now, and I'll love you always, my beautiful girl. I'll see you soon." With that, she reached out and pushed her daughter's arm away. Thea did the only thing she could; she ran towards the room.

Thea's heart was in her mouth. What should she do now? Her mum was in the hands of Daniel, she needed to get to the old witch. On top of having to find a way to save her boyfriend, things had gotten a bit too hard a bit too quickly.

She paced the room back and forth, hoping something would come to her.

"Any time now, guys would help," she spoke out loud to the elements, but nothing happened. "Great, so, when I actually need you, you're not there. Great bloody guardians you are!" she screamed at nothing. "I'm meant to be this all-powerful witch, but I have no clue what I'm meant to be doing. I can barely protect myself," she sobbed. "My magic only seems to work in emergencies; that's useless to me." She took a big gulp of air. "This is an emergency," she shouted again. "Please," she whispered as she fell to her knees.

Her hair fell out of its bun and covered her eyes. She had nothing on her that was of any use; she didn't even have her phone. But in all honesty, who would she call. She tucked her feet underneath her and just sat in the centre of the room; she felt hopelessly lost.

"We are not allowed to help you, Isamcey, but we can advise you on which way to go," the water element spoke to her kindly. The voice came out of nowhere.

"I'm lost. What am I going to do?" she cried.

"Your mother gave you a good starting point; following her plan is what we suggest," the voice said.

"But I don't even know how to get out of this building. The door will be guarded by now," she felt helpless.

"Yes, but that is not the only door in this room," Air said. Thea jumped up.

"Not the only door?" she looked around the room. Another door must be here somewhere.

"This room has always, and will always provide Isamcey

155

with whatever she needs," the voice said again. "You just have to will it so."

Thea felt a flood of excitement crash into her. She had everything she needed right here; she just had to work out how to get it.

"Okay, okay, okay, I can do this," she breathed. "Believe in yourself, just once, Thea, just once," she begged herself. "I need a way to the old witch, Mary," she thought. She prayed; she did everything she could think of.

Heart pounding, palms sweating, she sneaked just one eye open. Not daring to hope, but there it was, right in front of her, on the back wall. A door she had never seen before. It was simple wood, nothing fancy, no pretty ornate decorations, nothing, just plane iron hinges and a big old style, round iron door handle.

"Thank you," she didn't know who she was thanking, but she did it anyway.

She half skipped and half walked over to the door. Turning the handle and stepping through the door was harder than she thought it would be. She was scared, nervous, and excited but mostly determined to get this done. Too many people she loved were in danger.

"There's nothing left for it now," she told herself and pulled the door open. She stepped through before she could talk herself out of it.

Pressure was all around her; it was immense. She felt like she was being pulled and pushed in every direction all at the same time. Just when she thought she couldn't handle it any more it was over.

Trees surrounded her everywhere. She turned, yet more trees. She looked up, but she couldn't see their leafy tops; she looked down and saw nothing but earth.

"Oh… my… lord," every sense was assaulted all at once. The rich earthy smell was so strong she thought she might pass out. The sound of the leaves rustling in the wind was so loud, it was as if they were trying to deafen her. The strange green light that was emitted through the trees did odd things to her eyes. It was all a bit too much. She breathed slowly and began walking in the direction she was facing; it was the only option she had.

She had never been here before, so she had nothing to go on. All she knew was she had to find the old witch's hut. That was it; not a lot to go on, really. So, she just walked.

Time stood still while she trudged through the damp earth. She couldn't tell if it was morning or afternoon, just that she was lost in a wood with no way out. All she could do was keep wandering in hopes of bumping into the exact person she was looking for. The likelihood of that was very slim.

"Great plan, Thea, throw yourself into a wood with no way of knowing where you are or how to get home, another brilliant idea, well done," she mocked herself in a Valarie kind of way. She even began to miss that evil girl; at least if Valarie were there trying to humiliate her, she would know the way home.

"Oh, Jason. What have I got myself mixed up in?" she found that she pretended to be talking to her old best friend a lot nowadays.

As she continued to walk, it grew darker and colder, she was tired and it had begun to rain. Thea was numb; she didn't care any more how cold or wet she was, she didn't care that her legs hurt and her trainers let the water in. She was about to give up and just curl up into a ball when she was sure she could smell smoke. Her head whipped up and tried to follow the smell, but it kept disappearing.

"No, no, please, I need to find Mary. Please, I need her," she begged no one in particular. And when she looked up again, in the distance was a little old hut with smoke billowing out the chimney.

Thea could have cried, she tried to run but her legs kept giving out, she stumbled and fell a few times. She didn't care because she was going to get to that hut one way or another, be that on her feet or on her knees.

The door opened as she neared, and an old woman stuck her head out.

"Hello, Thea, I have been waiting for you," the old woman smiled kindly.

Thea couldn't believe her eyes. She was on her knees in the mud gazing up into the very first face she had ever laid eyes on. The image slammed into the front of her mind; she remembered seeing Mary for the very first time. She looked exactly the same now as she did then.

"Ladies, please help our guest; she has had a trying day," Mary told them. Two younger women came out and helped Thea to her feet. They half walked; half carried her through the door.

"She's waking up. Quick, get Mary," a female voice said.

Footsteps sounded all around her. She was fully awake but was a bit scared to open her eyes. She used her other senses to see if she could gauge anything.

The smell of herbs was so strong that it assaulted her nose. She couldn't resist wrinkling it; it was that or she rubbed her nose, and that would definitely give her away. She must have passed out as soon as she was taken into the old hut. She was sure she could remember there being at least three people with her. She may be wrong; there might be more.

The room was oddly quiet. No sounds had been made since

the female voice went to fetch Mary. Thea was getting anxious; she knew she would have to face whatever was on the other side of her eyelids sooner or later.

"One, two, three, open your eyes," she coached herself. Thea threw he eyes open and screamed. Two faces were gathered so closely around her. She tried to scramble back, but there was nowhere to actually go. Her heart pounded. She must have looked like a dear caught in headlights staring back at the two other women.

"It's okay, Thea, you are safe here," said a voice she vaguely remembered.

"M... Mary?" she stammered.

"The one and only, my dear," chuckled the old woman. "I have waited a long time to see you again, and what a treat it is to see you," she grinned at her.

Mary sat in a chair not far from the bed.

"Uh, Mary, can I have some space? Your friends are a bit too close," she asked in a nervous voice. Mary belly laughed.

"Oh, my dear, I'm sorry, girls move back; Thea needs some space to breathe," she ordered her friends to move away.

Thea smiled her thanks. She finally took in the room properly. The roof was low and made of tightly knitted leaves and branches. The walls were pretty much the same, they had animal hides and other kinds of handmade decorations hung from them, though. There were jam jars hanging from the ceiling by thick pieces of string with candle stubs placed within each one; all at different stages of use.

The bed Thea was laid on was incredibly comfortable. Half her blankets were animal hides the others were handmade from coarsely made yarn, but they were warm nonetheless. Turning her head, she saw an old, crudely made fireplace. Around the edges hung bunches of dried herbs and other things. Thea didn't care to know the origin.

"Is my home up to your standards, young Miss?" Mary was only teasing.

"Yes, sorry," Thea's cheeks flushed.

"No need, dear. Now, we have a lot to talk about, don't we?" she stared Thea in the eye, all sign of jest gone.

Thea looked from Mary then to the others in the room.

"Ah yes, quite right, dear. Ladies, on with your chores please, she's not going anywhere yet, so you can spend time with her later." Mary shooed the other girls away. Thea watched them leave. "You have grown into so much more than I ever thought possible, my girl. You are marvellous." Awe shone though Mary's voice.

"My lord, she is crazy. What was I thinking coming here?" Thea was getting worried. Mary was looking at her very oddly.

"Ha-ha, I'm not crazy, child, just pleasantly surprised," she told her.

"Oh no, she's reading my mind too!" Thea panicked. This only made Mary laugh more

"Then shut your mind off from me, stop projecting like you're a movie screen," she couldn't help but laugh; Thea was funny to watch. "I have waited a very long time to see you again," Mary smiled at her.

"Why?" Thea didn't understand. How did she know Thea was ever going to be here again? She knew she was born here, but that didn't mean she would ever come back.

"You're a very special girl, Thea. Don't you already know?" Thea felt her stomach drop. "I take it you are aware something is different with you then," Mary was able to gauge from the look on her face.

"I have only known about magic for a couple of weeks. Everything is so new," she said. "Everyone seems to want something from me. On top of that, the elements keep calling me Isamcey, and I just don't get it. Why me?" Mary was staring at her oddly. Thea felt like she was being scrutinised.

"What?" she practically barked at the old woman.

"Isamcey, you say?" Mary mused, her old wrinkled hand massaging the small of her back. "Much more than even I predicted... but very right, too... yes, Isamcey indeed," she spoke but as if to someone else, not to Thea.

"Uh, yeah, I hear all these things that I'm meant to be, but I don't even know how to control my power, let alone be this chosen one," she burst out. "Don't you get it? I was thrust into this world mere weeks ago. I had to start from the beginning, with a ticking time bomb placed above my head. I'm only seventeen. I just want to be a normal boring old teenager," she wined. "I met this guy, and he is amazing, he means the world to me, yet he's been ripped away by the people who were supposed to protect me. Now they have my mother too. It's too much. What am I meant to do?" she pleaded, everything tumbled out, followed by a flood of tears.

"Child, start from the beginning so I can try and understand what is going on here. Who were you with? Who was meant to protect you? Who has your mother and your friend? Then we can start to work out what to do," Mary instructed kindly.

Thea looked up, steadying her gaze on the old woman.

"The Brockmoor's, the Willow's and the Nightshades," she said without looking away. "Now, do you understand my plight?"

Chapter 14

Three days had passed since Thea arrived at Mary's. Three very long, slow days.

The old woman was keen to teach her everything she needed to know, everything she had missed from the very beginning, but her pace was too slow. Thea needed to get to Ryder and her mother, but Mary insisted on doing things properly, as she put it.

Most of the time, she was made to sit and focus on her inner power, to feel where her power stemmed from, to fully grasp what it meant to be a witch.

Mary had droned on about the origins of power, the different types of power, how they all worked in a different way, and how to best use them. Yet she hadn't once shown Thea a spell or a hex that would help her find her loved ones.

Every day that passed was a day further away from them, and it was killing her inside. She appreciated everything Mary had done for her, and she loved to hear the memories she had of her mother, but right now, all she really wanted to do was leave.

She had made up her mind. She was going to tell Mary she was leaving today whether she liked it or not.

She found the old woman behind the hut in the herb garden. "Mary, I need to leave today. I can't afford to lose any more time. God knows what they're doing to my mum and Ryder. I need to find them," she told her

"I see, and what do you plan to do when you get there, my dear," she questioned her.

Thea hated when she was made to feel stupid, and that was exactly what Mary was doing.

"Whatever needs to be done," was her simple reply.

"You may be Isamcey, child, but you know basically nothing of your power. How do you hope to even get there?" Mary rose her eyebrows to her.

"Look, lady, I got to you, didn't I?" she spat, not intending to be so rude.

"Hmm, with your mother's guidance, I might add," she pointed out.

"Then help me!" Thea yelled. "All this sitting around is doing nothing."

Mary stopped what she was doing and looked up at her

"Nothing you say, all that nothing you have been doing has been teaching you how to control your power, and my child, don't you need it," she paused. "Yes, I will help you, but girl, you need to learn some respect, I may be just an old woman to you, but I can assure you I was formidable in my days. You would be wise to listen carefully to me," she warned her. "You want to find your love and your mother, yes?" she probed,

"Yes," Thea replied meekly

"Well then, child, first you need to form a plan of action." She started a list of things to do "First, you need to decide which one you intend to go after first and how you plan to get there. Second, you need to decide how you will get in and find your loved ones. And third, what you will do when trouble arises," she stated. "What do you plan to take with you? How do you plan to carry it all? What do you plan to use as transport?" she continued. "The three covens are not housed close together, my dear. They are at constant war; it would not bode well for anyone if they were neighbours," she pointed out to Thea.

"Okay, fine, you have made your point. I'm horrifically under-prepared," Thea sulked; all she wanted was to see her mother's face again and to be held by Ryder.

"Lucky for you that you've got me then, isn't it, missy?" Mary smiled at her as she walked past. "Come on, child, we have a lot to do before we head out if you plan to leave anytime soon," she called over her shoulder.

It was amazing how agile that old lady was. She looked to be at least eighty, yet she was able to move around as swiftly as a cat when she wanted to.

The other women that resided with Mary were apparently her apprentices, but they only ever seemed to cook and clean. Thea didn't see that as very good work for an apprentice. They were nice enough, though; their names were Adele and Jessica. She had spent a little time talking with them the night she arrived; they were so excited to have her there. Mary had to give them extra chores just so Thea could have a rest from the endless tirade of questions they kept throwing at her.

They were busy in the small kitchen housed at the back of Mary's hut. They were drying herbs and hanging them by the fire when the pair entered the room.

"Ladies, I need you to help me gather up enough supplies for Thea and me for a good week or so. We will be leaving when the moon is at its highest," she told them. Adele looked as if she was going to protest but thought better of it.

"But gran…" Jessica went to say, but Adele hushed her.

"What's wrong?" Thea asked.

"I haven't left this hut in many years, Thea. They are concerned for my safety is all; the thing all you youngsters seem to forget is what I am capable of," she grinned. "Have faith in me, Isamcey, and you will be surprised," was all she said before she went about busying herself with packing.

Mary bade her apprentices farewell as she slung her pack over her shoulder. Thea followed suit as she stepped out into the cool night air. The woods were so different at this time of night. Everything took on a different look and feel.

Thea tugged at the heavy woollen cloak Mary had given her. It helped to shield her from the cold night air

"I look the part now," she chuckled to herself. "All I'm missing is the broom and hat," she had to grin as she thought of what old Maggie's face would have looked like if she saw her now.

The darkness was so vast up ahead. She was grateful that she hadn't gone on her own; there was no doubt in her mind that she would be hopelessly lost by now.

The two walked in silence for a while as they passed under the constant canopy of leaves. The leafy roof added to the feeling of being closed within a rather large box. It was like they were walking forever but getting nowhere. Their surroundings never seemed to change.

Thea's mind started to wander as they trudged on. She thought about Ryder and where he might be, what he might be going through and how he must be feeling. Sadness engulfed her; all she could see was his beautiful eyes full of pain. God knows what was happening to him. She hadn't seen him for almost a week now, yet it felt like longer. She had to force her mind elsewhere; thinking about him was hurting more than she could allow right now. She needed her mind to be clear and sharp. Not clouded by emotions.

The wind picked up every now and then as if it were in time with a silent melody that she could not hear. Aimlessly following Mary, she pulled at the ends of her hair. It was starting to annoy her how it kept flapping around and smacking her in the face.

"Bloody hell, why can't the wind just sod off for a bit? I can't see," she grumbled. And with that, the world became calm; the wind died down to a very gentle breeze that didn't ruffle her hair.

"You certainly do have some powers, don't you, child?" Mary called back to her; she could hear the old woman laughing up ahead.

"What do you mean?" Thea shouted a little too loudly.

"You have the elements at your every command. I have not seen the wind do as it is told so easily for a very, very long time," she remarked as she looked head, "I think this trip is going to be an interesting one at the very least."

The morning sun had just begun its ascent when the pair slowed their pace. Mary looked old, but she was relentless when it came to their walking speed. She set the pace; you either kept up or were left behind.

"We will rest here for a while. We made good time through the night; you did better than I thought you would," she proclaimed.

"Umm, thanks, I think," Thea replied. "What is the plan, Mary?" Thea asked gingerly

"That's up to you dear. You need to tell me who you want to go after first," she said steadily. "I won't tell you what to do or what to choose. I'm just here to guide you and teach you along the way," she pointed out.

"I know, but I don't know who to seek out first, who needs me the most," Thea was torn and she hated it. "My mum is my mum; she means the world to me, I love her like no other, but I get the feeling she can look after herself. Not that Ryder couldn't, it's just she was taken by Daniel, a warlock of the Brockmoor coven. Whereas Ryder, I fear, has been given over to the

Nightshade coven. And god knows what they are doing to him," her voice wobbled as she spoke the last few words.

"Well then, my dear, I think you have answered your own question, don't you?" She waited for Thea's reply, but she didn't get one. Thea was lost in thought, and she was okay with that. Mary got out her sleeping things and laid them out on the floor. The movement got Thea's attention.

"Wait, we can't sleep now; we have to get to Ryder," she urged Mary. She didn't want to waste time on aimless things like sleeping.

"We all need sleep. I suggest you do the same. We will only be here a couple of hours; trust me, you're going to need it. You won't get much more for quite a while," Mary told her.

"Fine, but please, only a couple of hours," she replied as she slumped down to the damp earth and dragged her make-shift sleeping bag out of her pack.

She grumbled the whole time about not being tired and hating the time-wasting. Within minutes she was snoring.

"Up, up, up, girl, we need to get moving before we lose too much of the light," Mary poked her with her walking stick. Thea moaned; she dragged herself up and brushed the tangled mess of hair out of her eyes.

The sun had begun its descent across the sky, and they had slept longer than they had intended. Thea yelped and scrambled to grab all her stuff.

She hated camping as a kid; she could never get all her sleeping things back into the ridiculously small bag provided.

"Ugh, I miss my bed, I miss my home, I miss my old life," she whined.

"Stop your moaning and just get on with it, sheesh, kids these days don't have a clue what hardship is like," Mary shook her head as she busied herself with her own packing. She made it look easy.

Finally, they were moving again. If not as fast this time. Thea was bogged down with tiredness. She hadn't gotten any real restful sleep, so felt worse for the rest than before.

Mary, on the other hand, looked spritely for her old age. Her perfect silver hair was held back by a single piece of string. Thea had watched her expertly whip it up into a neat little bun at the nap of her neck. It was all held in place with a twig she had found on the floor. No signs of tiredness showed on her weathered old face. She assured Thea that she felt as fresh as a daisy.

"So, my dear, why don't you tell me all about this young man we are going to rescue," she asked inquisitively,

Thea looked at her and beamed.

"Okay, well, his name is Ryder, he is almost nineteen years old, and he is beyond gorgeous," she gushed. "He's really tall, like at least easily a foot and a half taller than me."

She carried on describing Ryder in every in-depth detail she could. Mary just nodded and agreed in all the right places.

"Right, so I can now adequately imagine what he looks like from his head to his toes, but what is he like?" she asked Thea once more. She didn't need to know how dreamy his eyes were and how amazing his hands felt when they held hers. She wanted to know what he was like, what his personality was like, how he acted, how he treated Thea, and what his background was.

"Oh, yeah, sorry," Thea blushed; she had gotten so swept up in describing him she hadn't really listened to what she had been asked.

"He's kind, Mary, one of the only people who liked me for me, not just my power," she paused, lost in thought. She clearly missed him; Mary could see this. "As for his background and where he came from, well, I don't really know much, but what I do know is he is originally from the Nightshade coven," she shot a glance at Mary; she didn't show even one flicker of movement. "Before you say it, yes, I know they're not a great bunch of people, but Ryder is different. He got away from there; he didn't want to be like his family," she let the words rush out. Somehow, she felt she needed to defend him. "He doesn't agree with their ways. He treats me like I'm the most important person in the world, and I miss him," she sobbed, she didn't realise she had let her feeling out, but clearly, she had.

"But you are the most important person in the world, Thea. You are Isamcey," Mary stated.

"I don't care. He didn't even know that, though. I found out after he was gone," Thea sniffed. "I know you're probably thinking I'm just a child; what do I know about feeling and things, but what I do know is, it doesn't matter how old I am, the way I feel is awful, and I can't bear to think of my life without him in it, so right now I don't have any other choice than to throw myself further into the unknown, in hopes that I can find a way to get to him," she said, she hadn't truly admitted to herself how she felt about the boy she hardly knew, but it felt good to finally realise it.

"Love is a funny thing, it works in strange ways, and it certainly doesn't take age into account, so no, dear, I don't think you're a child that has no clue about love; by the sounds of things, it has already found you and right now you are fighting its cause." She patted Thea on the back. "Come on then, let's get moving. We have a lover boy to rescue."

Thea had to laugh as she watched Mary bow her head and march on.

Thea had so much she wanted to ask the older witch; she just didn't know where to start.

"I can hear your thoughts," Mary called back. "Ask away. We have nothing better to do while we walk," she said.

"Uh, that right there. How do I learn to block people from my mind? Nothing is sacred any more," Thea asked as she plodded on.

"It's simple, dear. Just imagine pulling a great big sheet up around your mind, all the way round, though. You can't leave any gaps," she instructed. "Go on, try it now, and I'll see if I can hear your thoughts," she challenged her.

Thea did just that. She exhaled and concentrated on pulling the sheet around her mind, just like Mary had told her.

"Go on, try now," she called. She could feel something tugging at the sides of her mind like it was prodding and poking, trying to find a way in.

"Ah ha, you left a tiny gap. I got ya," Mary's voice laughed into her mind.

"Damn it, let me try again she called out. They worked at it for a good few hours until Thea had fully mastered cloaking her mind.

Once Mary was through with her, she could block anybody from her thoughts. She was so proud of herself. She wished she could show off her new skills to Ryder.

She tried to distract her mind by asking Mary about herself, about her life before she knew her. But whenever she prodded her for information, the old woman would expertly skirt off onto a new topic.

"Mary, how old are you?" she absentmindedly asked her as she kicked the leaves up from the beaten down earth with her very worn-out looking trainers.

"What a question to ask a lady," Mary scoffed back.

"Sorry, I didn't mean it in a rude way," Thea apologised. "Sheesh, she wants to know everything about me, but I can't ask one question about her," she thought to herself.

"Let's just say I'm much older than you think, and I have seen a lot more of the world and its happenings than most people," was Mary's answer.

"Hmm. So, where did you come from then?" she tried to pry. Mary took a while to answer.

They were still passing through the endless forest. A slight incline had hindered them for the last hour or so. Surely they will come to the top of this hill shortly?

"I'm from everywhere, dear; I have lived everywhere and seen pretty much everything," but she didn't see the person dressed all in black drop down from the trees right onto their path before it was too late.

Energy gathered so fast at the edge of Thea's fingertips it shocked her; she hadn't even tried to call it forth. Her fingers were doing the tale-tale tingling thing they did when the elements were involved. She readied herself for anything. Not that she had any clue what she was going to do; she just hoped it would come to her at the time.

"Who are you? What are you doing here?" demanded the person dressed in black.

Mary looked him up and down, then looked back at Thea. She hid her smile when she saw what Thea was doing; she was impressed that she could be action-ready so quickly.

"Put that thing away before you poke someone's eye out," she scolded the person in front of them.

He was holding a full wooden staff out in front of them, pointing it straight at Mary's chest. He didn't quite know what to do with that answer; normally, there would be a fight or an easy surrender. Not an old woman telling them off.

"Oh, for goodness sake, I taught your grandparents everything they knew, so there is nothing you can do that I can't outwit. Now put that thing away, don't make me ask you twice," she barked at him. "While you're at it, lead me to Samren; you can explain to her why you were flapping a stick in my face." With that, Mary walked past the person blocking their way moments before, as if nothing had happened.

"Well, hurry up. I haven't got all day," she shouted back at them.

"Unbelievable!" Thea released the energy she had been holding and laughed as she rushed to catch up with her new mentor.

Chapter 15

Hushed voices whispered from the shadows, from above and below, as Thea made her way through the tangle of rope bridges that intertwined with the trees themselves. The view would have been breath-taking if she wasn't so damned scared of slipping and falling to her death.

Small wooden houses and shelters had been built all along the treetops among the branches of dozens of massive trees. They looked as if they had been here a while too. The leaves of the top branches formed natural roofs for the dwellings.

Thea followed Mary along yet another bridge that wound its way upwards. She couldn't quite believe what had happened. One minute she was standing on the edge of a hilltop following Mary and asking her questions, then the next minute, she was stepping off the hill and onto apparently nothing, which turned out to be the first bridge in the very intricate maze that served as the pathways to a hidden community. Which Mary clearly knew.

"Welcome to the Hidden Balcony," Mary proclaimed. Thea just followed on in silence. She had too much to concentrate on to answer.

Once they had eventually finished climbing trees, Thea allowed herself to relax a little. Mary had met with her old friend Samren. She was one of the elders of this small coven. Apparently, Mary had helped them establish their home, and they owed her a lot.

Thea stuck out like a sore thumb. She couldn't help but

notice everyone staring at her and whispering behind their hands. It was so unnerving that she shuffled closer to Mary, who was in talks with her old friend.

"Yes, I understand, but what I don't think you are hearing is our urgency, Samren. We need to use your portal so that we can drastically cut our travel time; so much is at stake here," Mary pushed the issue.

"You know as well as me that the portal is old, plus it is to only be used by one person and one person alone; until they show themselves, then no, it will not be opened. Not even for you, my dear old friend," Samren wouldn't budge.

She was very old herself, not as old as Mary, of this Thea was sure. She had long wispy white hair, and her skin seemed to hang on her in delicate paper-like folds. Her eyes were the colour of cloudy glass, and her legs were too frail to hold her up. She was seated in a chair made purely of intertwined branches and leaves. Mary took a deep calming breath.

"Thea, dear, step forward, please," she encouraged the younger girl. "Now, you may need to shout; her hearing isn't what it used to be," Mary informed her.

"What do I say?" she whispered out the side of her mouth while trying to smile politely at the old lady in front of her.

"Oh, sorry, yes, you need to call forth the elements all at the same time and prove to her you are the one they have been waiting for," Mary winked at her. "Go on then, get on with it," she nudged Thea on the hip with her walking stick.

"Ouch, Mary?" nerves smashed into her. She hadn't had to call the elements on demand before; they sort of just came to her, not the other way around. "No pressure then, huh?" she mumbled. Thought after thought ran through her head. She didn't know what to do.

174

She looked over at her mentor and saw her slowly nod at her. She stilled her racing heart and found the focus that Mary had taught her for days. She found her centre and reached out to her elemental friends.

"Earth, water, fire and air, I call you now to my side. Will you aid me in my task? Please grace me with your presence," she chanted. She exhaled and opened her eyes. Her ears were greeted by a chorus of shocked gasps and mummers of awe.

"Hello, Isamcey," the four elements greeted her as one. She smiled at them.

"Hello, my friends," she smiled back. "I give you permission to make yourselves comfortable I know how you dislike the closeness," she told them. With that, they spread out along her outstretched arms to allow themselves some space.

"So, it is true. The time has finally come." Samren's croaky voice pierced through the thick silence.

"Now do you believe me?" Mary asked, a little too smugly. Samren bowed her head to Thea,

"Isamcey, the use of the ancient portal is yours. Use it wisely as it is unpredictable; it has not been used in hundreds of years. Go carefully," she said still with her head bowed. "And may you show favour to us in the coming times," she concluded.

Thea was worse than lost for words. What do you say to an elderly leader of a coven who was bowing to you?

"Umm, thank you for your help," was all that she managed to stutter out before Mary jumped in and saved her, leading her away towards those terrible rope bridges once more. At least they were leading down this time.

The ground was definitely where Thea felt at her happiest. It was beautiful up amongst the trees, but it wasn't an experience she wanted to partake in again any time soon.

She walked beside Mary on legs that felt like jelly. They wove around a good many trees until they came to one tree in particular. It was ancient, all gnarled and knotted with moss covering a good proportion of it. Set deep within its trunk was what Thea thought looked like deep scratches and grooves. They turned out to be magical runes.

"This is the portal, Thea; it will speed up our travel time immensely," Mary stated. "Now all you have to do is put a bit of your blood on that there rune, and the portal will re-open. There will only be a short time for us to go through it, so no dilly-dallying, you hear me?" she spoke sternly to her as if she was making sure an unruly child did as they were told.

"My blood? How on earth do I get my blood into that tree?" she hadn't even finished speaking when Mary, as quick as light, was out with her hand and nicked her finger.

"Ouch, Mary, for goodness sake, stop hurting me," she scowled at her.

"Stop your moaning. I solved your problem, didn't I? Now rub your damn finger on the rune like I showed you so we can get going." She almost prodded her once more but thought better of it.

Thea stepped up to the tree and placed her finger exactly where Mary showed her. At first, nothing happened; she looked behind her and shrugged. Then the loudest whirling noise erupted from the middle of the tree trunk. Leaves, twigs, and all kinds of debris were being pulled into the swirly bluey-green vortex.

"Jump, child, we don't have time to admire it," Mary placed her hand on Thea's back and shoved her through the portal. She didn't have any choice in the matter.

Everything swam around her as she fell through the portal. All she could see was a great mass of moving and twisting blue and green lights. The odd twig would fly past her head every now and then too. Never in her life had she ever experienced anything so surreal. Time was indistinguishable; she couldn't tell how long she had been inside it or where she was going to end up. All she knew was she was starting to feel a bit sick from all the spinning. She was sure she could hear Mary behind her, but she couldn't work out how to turn around to see.

It didn't last too long though before the hard, unforgiving floor suddenly jumped out of nowhere to greet her.

"Ugh," she cried, and her head banged off the hard earth.

She felt her leg get shredded as she scrapped it along the ground. This was instantly followed by a harsh stinging pain, joined by a hot wet feeling. She barely wanted to look. She hated blood.

Mary had landed a little way off from her. She was already sitting when Thea had found her.

"Mary, you all right?" she called over to her.

"Fine child, are you hurt," she called back

"Yes, but I don't know how badly. I'm too afraid to find out," she admitted.

"I'm coming, don't worry," and Mary was there before she knew it.

Thea braved a quick glance at her leg. Her jeans were ruined, that was for sure, and there was a great deal of blood. Mary assured her it was just a surface wound and that she would have her fixed up in no time.

"Right, lay back. This is going to sting," Mary warned her.

Thea braced herself, but she couldn't stifle the scream for long. Mary had dug something out of her pack and was applying it to Thea's leg.

Sting was an understatement. Sheer agony was more like it.

"Oh, shush, you big baby, it will stop in a minute," she teased the girl, but she was right, the pain did ease to practically nothing within minutes, and Thea was up and walking once more.

"Where are we?" she asked, standing with her hands on her hips; she looked around her.

"Well, if I'm not mistaken, we are not far from your young man," she said. "This is the outskirts for one of the Nightshades estates."

Mary had to pretty much hold Thea back from racing off in the direction of Ryder. She wasn't aware of how dangerous this place was and how careful they had to be.

They needed to plan everything down to the last tiny detail if they wanted to get out of this alive.

"Hold your pretty little horses, Missy; we can't just charge off in there like we own the place. You have no idea who you are dealing with," Mary stopped her before she disappeared.

"But Ryder is there; we can't waste any time." She practically was begging.

"You thought the council of the Brockmoor coven were bad; they are nothing more than cute fluffy little bunnies compared to this lot. We do this my way, Isamcey or not at all. I won't let you get yourself killed," she said with finality. "Plus, have you seen yourself? You look almost as bad as the walking dead; you can't walk in there like that."

Thea looked down at herself. She really did look a mess. The best part of her jeans was ripped and hanging open. Her top was torn and stained. It wasn't even worth trying to work out what her hair resembled, but from what she could feel, it wasn't good.

"That was my favourite pair of jeans as well," she really felt like stamping her foot in protest but knew she would just look downright stupid.

"We will have to walk back out and towards the nearest town. You need new clothes; we both do," Mary was already walking in the opposite direction. Thea knew better than to protest. You either followed or got left behind.

"Are we there yet?" Thea moaned, dragging her feet along behind her.

"You know you sound like a five-year-old, right?" Mary mocked her.

"I don't care. We have been walking for hours, it's cold and my leg hurts," she sulked.

"Children nowadays don't have a clue about hardship," the old woman muttered to herself again. It was fast becoming one of her new favourite sayings.

"Well, frankly, I don't know why we have to go about everything the hard way. Would it kill you to try things the easier way?" Thea grumbled

"Oh, please do elaborate," Mary was in the mood to tease her, apparently.

"Okay then, for instance, why do you have to live in the middle of nowhere?" she said with a matter-of-fact tone. "Like honestly, Mary, have you never heard of simple home comforts? Such as running water, indoor plumbing, electric lights." She listed them off on her fingers. "Proper beds, real duvets, oh how I miss my bed. A simple radiator instead of a crude fire! And an oven! You would love an oven!"

Mary looked back at her like she was crazy.

"A car!" she practically shouted at her "We could have gotten to Ryder and back by now if we had a car."

Mary stopped her before she could prattle on about another thing

"Enough, I have heard enough," she held up her hand right in front of Thea's face; she was a little taken aback.

"Fine, there is no need to be rude," she said, crossly folding her arms.

"I am not rude, young lady. I have just heard enough of your drivel; all these so-called home comforts have made you lazy and weak. It would never have been this way when I was your age," Mary stated.

"I am not lazy! Thank you very much, and I am certainly not weak," Thea was growing angry.

"You are lazy. I bet you can't even call a simple witch light or light a fire with your base magic! And I don't mean with the help of the elements! I mean by yourself." She had fully stopped and had her hands on her hips, staring the young girl down.

Heat rose to Thea's cheeks, her hair ruffled around her head, and her bluey green eyes were set in a piercing stare.

"You're wrong," she growled.

Mary could feel a change in the air. The crude path they were walking along had wound its way back through a thick patch of forest which was beginning to thin out now, the trees were becoming less and less, and the sun had risen higher in the sky. Yet they were still adequately covered.

"Prove it then, little girl, you are meant to be the all-powerful Isamcey, yet all I have seen is the elements doing it all for you and a hell of a lot of whining," Mary knew she had pushed Thea's buttons, she knew she was forcing her hand.

Thea glared at her. All she had heard since entering this new world was criticism, and she'd had enough. If she wanted to see what Thea could do, then she would damn well show her.

The air crackled and fizzed with energy; both of them could feel it. Thea barely moved her fingers, but she dragged all that pulsing energy to her. She felt it gather around her fingertips, her toes, arms, and head.

Her angry eyes never left the old lady's face.

"Fine, you want to see what I can do; I'll show you," Thea warned.

She lifted her hand, ready to prove her point. The trees had stilled; the wind refused to blow, and the birds were silent.

"Stop!" Mary boomed. "I can feel your power. I just needed to force you to feel it, too. You need to start believing in yourself, girl, as I'm not going to be around much longer," she proclaimed. "I can't go much further with you. I can't cross their borders. If I did, then the danger you would be in would be catastrophic," Mary sighed.

Thea dropped her hands to her sides.

"What do you mean? I can't go in there alone; I have no clue what I'm doing," she panicked.

"Yes, you can. You are a force to be reckoned with, my girl. You just have to know you can do it and believe you will succeed," she sighed. "I was only meant to show you the way, not do it for you," she concluded. "You must move quickly now, or you will be caught; no doubt that amount of energy surging in one place at the same time will have been detected. It won't be long until this place is brimming with Nightshade members." She smiled sadly at her. "You need to just keep heading in that direction, it won't be long and the compound will come into view," Mary pointed down the path they had been travelling.

Thea frantically looked around; she was scared and nervous and something else altogether.

"You will be fine; I believe it with my whole soul." Tears glistened in the old witch's eyes. "Oh, it has been my greatest honour being a small part of your life," she said wistfully, then

181

she bowed to Thea and was gone.

"Mary!" Thea called her name, whirling around, but she was truly gone, nowhere to be seen,

"I thought we were going to get new clothes! Not lead me right to the door and leave!" she breathed; a tear left her eyes. "You crafty old thing, you could teleport this whole time," Thea had to smile despite the dread she felt in her stomach.

"I'm coming, Ryder," she spoke to the wind and set off down the path.

Chapter 16

The world seemed ten times bigger now she was alone.

Mary hadn't been wrong; it wasn't long until she could hear the distinct sound of voices.

She had left the relative cover of the forest a while ago, so there weren't many places to hide. Just off to her left was a low-lying hedge. She dove for it and crawled behind it.

Lying on her belly wasn't pleasant. The damp earth smelt so strong and her cut leg was stinging once more. She hardly dared to breathe, afraid her breath would betray her and give her away. She laid there for what felt like hours waiting for the voices to disperse. She couldn't look up to check. If she did, she might as well just hand herself straight over.

"Come on, the alarm was triggered from over there," said a gruff sounding voice. "If we come back empty-handed, Victor will be furious," the same voice said.

Thea listened intently, with her heart in her mouth. If she was caught, God knows what would happen.

Her leg had gone dead. It felt like a lead weight stuck to her body, and she needed to move. She twisted slightly and instantly regretted it; her jeans caught on something and ripped open a bit more. The wound on her leg began to bleed again; the hot searing pain raced up her leg with such speed, she couldn't help but gasp. She threw her hand over her mouth, hoping to stifle more sound from escaping.

"What was that?" one of the voices called out.

"What was what?" replied the other deep male voice.

"I heard something behind us," the voices had gotten louder.

"Damn it," she cursed.

Thea wriggled as far under the bush as she could, but she knew it wasn't going to do her any good. She had already alerted them to where she was.

Ryder slipped into her mind just then. She tried to think about what he would do if he was in her situation. But she came up blank.

All she could think about was how badly she wished he was with her. She felt like her heart actually ached.

"I miss you too," she heard his voice inside her head.

Thea practically jumped but caught herself before it was too late.

"Ryder, is that really you?" she called out with her mind. She didn't allow herself to really hope for a reply.

"Thea?" came the muffled surprised reply moments later. "I thought I was dreaming. Is that really you?" Ryder's smooth voice filled her mind. She could have cried. She never realised how much she missed hearing it.

"Where are you? Are you okay?" she didn't know what to ask first.

"I'm okay, but where the heck are you? You shouldn't be anywhere near here, Thea, it's not safe for you," his voice sounded desperate.

"Umm, well, actually, I don't know where I am, but I can't be too far if I'm able to hear you," she said back.

She thought about her surroundings in as much clarity as she could.

"Do you know this place?" she thought as she sent him the image in her mind. Her heart pounded so hard, she had missed him so badly, and she hadn't known how much until right then.

He was so close yet still so far.

"Oh no, Thea, you're right outside my father's estate. If they find you…" he trailed off.

"Ryder…Ryder," she shouted. All was silent; no reply came.

Two rough hands caught hold of her by the shoulders and yanked her upwards.

"What do we have here, then?" the first male voice said.

"Looks like we have found us a little trespasser," they both laughed.

"Victor will be please to meet you," they said as they dragged her down the path and towards the compound.

The sun had shown itself by the time Thea had reached the estate of this Victor person she kept hearing about. Its unforgiving rays shone down relentlessly onto her bare neck; no doubt it was burning.

Giant iron gates barred their way just up ahead. Cold and menacing, standing like two unmoving guards in front of them. Her two burly escorts walked either side of her, each holding one of her arms and neither one caring about the state of her leg; and how it hindered her as they dragged her along.

The guy to her left was very big, not just tall but stocky too. He had a perfectly shaven head and a small black goatee. His eyes were not all that kind, just like his hands and how tightly he held on to her.

The guy on her right was smaller but no more friendly to look at. He had greasy brown hair and horrible yellow teeth. Every time Thea would look over at him, he would snarl at her.

"Aren't you a pretty little thing," he sneered at her.

He made Thea feel sick. She chose to concentrate on her shoes as she walked along; they were the best-looking thing around here anyway.

"I wonder what Victor will do with you, hey," the greasy man laughed out loud.

"Ryder, are you there?" she called out in her mind. She needed him right now; she was so scared. She was meant to be there to rescue him, but once again, she needed him to save her. She didn't get a reply.

"Come on, little lady, time to meet the boss man," greasy hair said as the other one punched in a key code on the security pad.

The house in front of her was enormous. It looked like a beautiful old manor house. So many windows were spaced along the vast number of walls. Trailing vines crept along the whole of the front part of the house, all the way up to the upper levels, only ending just below the chimney breasts.

The sound of gravel crunching under their feet was loud and harsh on her ears; her senses seemed to be on overload right now. The lights all seemed too bright, the sounds too loud, and the smells too strong. Her escorts, if you could even call them that, stopped in front of the main entrance to the house. She heard greasy hair say something to the guys who stood at the doors, but Thea just couldn't focus on the words. She was starting to feel woozy, and the world had begun to spin.

"Catch her; she has lost a lot of blood. Take her straight to the infirmary; she needs to be looked at before Victor will see her," a new voice said before the blackness took her.

The sharp smell of disinfectant filled her nose, and the brightness of the surgical light shined down into her eyes. She could hear the faint beep, beep, beep of machines somewhere off in the distance. Moving her head was hard. It took a few moments to remember what had happened and where she was. She tried not to open her eyes too quickly; she wasn't sure who was in the room with her, if anyone. She couldn't hear the sounds of others, so she risked it.

She was laid out on a hospital bed in one of those awful, unflattering hospital gowns. Her leg ached a lot.

Slowly, she tried to sit up and glanced down at her leg. It had been cleaned, plus there were perfectly straight stitches where her leg had once gaped open. Looking around the room, she saw a new set of clothes folded neatly on the nearby chair. The room she was in was small, bright, and very clean. There was one small window on the left wall, but there were bars blocking her way to the outside. A white curtain had been pulled up around one side of the bed, obscuring her view of the rest of the room. She tried dragging her leg to the edge of the bed; that was a bad idea. The pain was instant and very intense; she wasn't going to try that again. She sat quietly for a while, thinking of any way out, but nothing seemed possible right now.

The door clicked open. Thea froze. The curtain was pulled back, revealing a young-looking woman dressed all in green.

"Ah, I see our patient is up. How do you feel?" she asked her kindly. Thea looked her up and down.

"Fine, I guess, apart from my leg. Where am I?" she asked back. Her voice was rough and felt like gravel when she spoke.

The new woman smiled as she moved towards her. Thea watched her carefully as she approached.

"Don't worry, I'm not going to hurt you; you did a pretty good job of that on your own," she laughed. "And to answer your question, you are in the infirmary in master Victor's house," the woman told her; her voice was full of admiration when she spoke the man's name. "Master Victor is waiting for you as we speak. I am to help you dress and show you the way to his study," she told

Thea as she checked her temperature and pulse. "All seems okay. Come on then, let's get you ready," she encouraged Thea.

Pulling her new clothes on was harder than she thought it would be. Her whole body was stiff, and moving her injured leg was not easy. With help from the nurse, she managed to pull the pale blue leggings on, one leg at a time and the simple white round neck t-shirt fit perfectly. She had to admit it felt amazing to be in clean clothes once again. Her hair had been washed for her when she had passed out. She found a simple elastic band sat on the side, which she snatched up and pulled her hair into a high pony tail, out of her face. Lastly, there was a brand-new pair of crisp white trainers waiting for her at the foot of her bed, and her eyes lit up.

The nurse kindly helped her get them on.

"My necklace," Thea asked frantically. "I had a necklace. It's not here now; I want my necklace," she demanded. The nurse looked uneasy.

"Uh well, I'm sure we will find it, don't worry," she muttered.

Thea wasn't happy, but what could she really do about it right now. She had promised her mum she would never take it off.

"When you find it, please, please make sure I get it back. It was a gift from my mother and holds a lot of sentimental value to me," Thea explained; the nurse just nodded.

"Right, I would say we are finally ready," she said to Thea. "Follow me, this way, please."

The walk from the infirmary was a challenge. Thea followed the nurse down a long corridor lined with old paintings and numerous different fine art. The ceilings were very high, with skylights built in at even intervals. This place was beautiful, but

Thea couldn't enjoy it; she was too nervous, and moving her leg took all her concentration.

"Here we are, dear, good luck," the nurse said as she left Thea at the door.

Thea looked around; she didn't know what to do other than knock. She lifted her hand, but before she could rap her knuckles on the door, she heard a scream, a horrible ear-splitting scream. One she had heard before.

"Ryder," she thought. Her face felt wet. A tear had escaped and run down her cheek. She knew the scream had been him; she just knew it. Pain for him and anger battled each other inside her. She had to find him, but there was no way she could do it like this. She had to be clever. She had to actually use her head, not go charging in and causing more trouble. So, she knocked.

"Enter!"

The man sitting behind the large wooden desk was not what she expected. He was willowy thin, with jet black hair slicked back from his forehead. He wore a perfectly clean, sharp-looking black suit and black tie. His long snow-white hands were folded neatly in front of him on top of the desk. He looked the perfect image of cool, calm and collected that you would expect of anyone in charge.

"Hello, young lady, it's lovely to finally meet you. Allow me to introduce myself," the man said. "I am Victor Peters, high councilman of the renowned Nightshade coven, and you are?" he said with such an air about him.

"Thea Jameson," was all she said. She hoped her voice didn't show how scared she truly was.

"Charmed, I'm sure," he rested his chin upon his finger. "You look familiar, my dear. Have we met before?" he asked her, all charming, but she wasn't fooled.

"No, I'm sure I would remember," Thea tried to sound sweet and innocent. That chilling scream she had heard outside ripped through the air once more. She whipped her head round; she knew she had to control her emotions; she couldn't allow this man to see she was affected.

"I'm sorry about the unpleasant noise. A certain member of our coven has to relearn the rules and laws that we adhere to; he seems to have misplaced his understanding," Victor spoke as if it was perfectly normal to hear the tortured screams of your victims, as if it was nothing.

Thea's hand shook. She hated knowing Ryder was in so much pain, and she was just stood there.

"So, let's discuss why you were skulking around outside my house, shall we?" Victor smiled at her, all pretence lost. He was down to business now. He looked scarily like Ryder when he wore his serious face.

"I was not skulking, actually," she tried to sound confident, her chin raised in the air.

"I see, so what were you doing then, inspecting the underside of my hedgerow?" he laughed, a sour sounding laugh at his own joke.

She searched her head for any kind of plausible answer.

"I was just," but she was cut off by the worst scream yet. "Ryder!" she gasped, unable to hold it back.

"Oh, I see now, you know my son. Bloody awful name his mother gave him, isn't it?" Victor said so flatly.

Thea shook all over; Victor just laughed.

"Yes, that is him making that awful racket. He's been at it for days now, resilient thing at least," he smirked at her. "Let me guess, you are one of the many floozies he met on his unauthorised little get away?" he paused for effect. "Well, he's home now and won't be leaving again, so you won't need to be worrying about him any more, will you?"

Victor was vile in Thea's eyes; she could see now why Ryder hated him so much.

"The only problem is what to do with you. You are clearly from the magical world, or you wouldn't have been able to find us and set off our alarms like you did," he pondered out loud. "What to do, what to do, hmm." He drummed his fingers on his chin.

"I can see why Ryder hates you. You're a vile excuse for a man," she spat at him, only hate burned behind her eyes. Everything about him oozed evil. She remembered Ryder explaining that his father had ascended. That he needed to drink blood to keep himself alive and to keep the vast amount of power he now controlled. She didn't doubt it for a second that this man – if you could even call him that any more – was anything but pure evil. Victor tore his eyes away from her and looked behind him, and nodded

"I think maybe my son could do with a break and a little visitor," he pushed himself up from his seat. "Jacob, please lead our charming little guest here to my son; he has a visitor.

Chapter 17

Jacob shoved Thea along the corridor. Victor was marching along in front; he seemed way too thrilled by the prospect of what was to come.

The walk to where Ryder was being held was full of twists and turns. Thea had hoped to memorise it so she could find her way back, but she lost count of the amount of left and right turns they had taken. She took note of how the floor gradually sloped downward, the air became cooler, and the walls were not quite so luxurious the further along they went. The last set of doors they passed were solid metal; not the pretty wooden doors like all the rest had been. Once the door had closed, the smell of blood, sweat and something else hit her full force, making her gag.

"A unique fragrance isn't it?" Victor laughed. "This way, dear, not far now."

Thea trembled as she stumbled along behind Victor. Ryder screamed once more. Thea refused to make a sound even though her eyes filled up with tears, and she bit down hard on her lower lip to stop them from falling. She would not give them the satisfaction of seeing how much this hurt her.

"Here we are, one moment please, I'll just check he is decent. I know how much he would hate it if he didn't look his best," Victor mocked before opening the door.

Thea heard him order whoever was inside to leave. Three men came lumbering out. They were covered in blood; well, it looked like blood at least.

"Son, you have a visitor," his father grinned at him. Now sit up straight, be polite," Victor barked. "Come in, dear," he called to Thea.

Ryder lay sprawled out on the floor, and his hair was matted to his head. It was no longer the dirty blond Thea knew; it was a mix of browns and blacks; it was caked in blood and filth. His face was unrecognisable, and his lip was split and bleeding. There was blood trailing from his nose. His right eye was puffy and swollen, and he couldn't open it. There were too many shades of blue, black and purple; it was hard to take it all in. His clothes were torn to shreds. The sight of him was so horrific.

"Let me go," Thea tried to shake Jacob off so she could get to him. Ryder looked up.

"No, Thea." He hung his head. "Father, please don't hurt her, do whatever you want to me, but not her," he begged.

Thea shook the oaf Jacob off her and dropped to the floor. Her hands reached Ryder first. Every touch pained him, but he didn't protest. Victor watched them in smug satisfaction.

"But my son, hurting her would be the best punishment for you," he sang.

"Father, please," Ryder was so quiet he almost didn't have a voice left. Victor just laughed.

"You know what, because I'm in such a giving mood, I will allow her to stay here with you for a while," he smirked. "Oh, but Thea dear, you must wear this." he wacked a black leather-looking cuff on her wrist." We can't have you doing any magic now, can we?" with that, he left, slamming the door behind him.

Thea hated him, and she seethed with loathing.

"You shouldn't have come," Ryder sobbed as he reached out his hand to touch her face. She couldn't hold the tears back any longer; they fell freely.

"What have they done to you?" she choked out. "You look awful," she continued.

"Oh, thanks. I doubt you would look much better in my position," he joked back. She laughed but cried at the same time.

"There's the jokester I love," she whispered as she moved closer to him.

"I love you too, princess," he mumbled into her hair.

She knew she shouldn't have felt so elated right then, in their current situation but hearing him say those three words was everything to her. Slowly they made their way towards the back wall. Every movement was hell for Ryder; they really had done a number on him.

"Listen to me, Thea, you have to get out of here. You can't stay," he urged her.

"I'm not leaving you here," she argued back.

"Yes, you are. If they do to you what they have done to me, I couldn't stand it. I wouldn't forgive myself," he pleaded with her. "How did you even find me anyway?" He paused. "After Dan cornered me back at Brockmoor, he made sure no one would be able to follow me; he had two of his little lackeys ship me back here. In all honesty they were more scared than me," he tried to laugh but it hurt too much. "You're going to be in so much trouble with the council when they find out you're gone," he continued. "I'll get the blame for that one, too," he grinned, causing his lip to crack open once more.

"Ouch, Ryder, be careful." She reached up and dabbed at his lip with the corner of her top.

He wrapped his uninjured arm around her and hugged her as tight as he could.

"I have missed you so much," he breathed.

She felt her heart swell with love for her very bruised

194

boyfriend.

"I knew you wouldn't just up and leave me," she sighed as she moved a little closer to him.

"Never, Thea, you are my everything," he stated. She loved him more right then.

"Brockmoor isn't safe any more," Thea explained. "Dan took my mother; I only just got away. He doesn't trust anyone, and he hates me," she told him. "I ended up with a woman called Mary," she knelt back down in front of Ryder. "I've got to tell you something," she looked at him; he understood she meant in his mind, as no doubt they were being watched. She took a deep breath, and she was nervous. She cleared her mind and reached out to him but she couldn't find her way. She didn't understand what was wrong.

"The cuff, Thea," Ryder tapped the leather bracelet thing on her wrist. "You can't do any form of magic."

"Oh," she looked around, "I bloody hate this place."

"Me too, don't say what you were going to say just in case, okay?" he whispered. She nodded. "I don't know how long my father will allow you to stay, probably not long. He knows it will hurt me more, and hurting me seems to be his new hobby!" he stated, looking around. "No doubt it's another one of his cruel jokes," he concluded.

"Well, let's just enjoy the time we have, for now, I will work out how to get us out of here, I promise," she meant it too.

"I wish I could take all this away and make you feel better." He tried to smile at her.

"Having you here is enough, but I do wish you weren't here; I know my father will do anything to hurt me, and the worst thing he could do to me is get his hands on you." he pulled her over for a proper hug. "Ah, ouch," he sucked in air.

"Sorry, sorry," she said, trying to pull herself away.

"No, it's worth it," he said as he closed his eye and breathed in the sweet smell of her hair and the feel of her next to him again. She sank into the feel of him and drifted off.

"Take her, leave him," barked a vaguely familiar voice. Before Thea had fully opened her eyes, she was being yanked from Ryder's arms.

"No, no, don't! Father, please don't. I'll do as you ask, I promise," Ryder yelled at his father as Thea was carted out of his cell. Victor didn't even grace him with a reply; he just stared blankly at him as he slammed the door in his son's face.

All Thea could hear as she was unwillingly escorted away was Ryder screaming her name, begging his father not to hurt her.

"Well, my dear, we have a very busy day for you today," Victor began as he walked behind her.

She was being dragged by two thuggish men; they had hold of her under each arm, and she didn't even bother trying to walk. She glared at Victor the whole way.

"First off, we need to clean you up, my son carelessly bled all over your clean clothes," Victor said in mock disgust. "He always was a careless boy," he added. "It was very sweet watching the two of you last night, might I add. He clearly cares for you more than he did any of the other girls he used to play with," Victor was trying to get to Thea, but she wasn't going to let him. "Then, after that, we must meet with a few of my fellow councilmen for a little chat," he went on. "I'm sure you're going to love them, seeing how well we have hit it off," still she didn't make a sound. "Then finally, if you have played nicely all day, I might let you join me when I go back to visit my son. We will have to see, won't we?" he spoke to her as if she was a child.

"Don't touch him," she finally said, loathing dripped from

every word.

"Ah, there is that beautiful voice I have been waiting to hear," he smirked at her. "Now, I'll make you a deal. Depending on how you participate today will depend on how Ryder gets treated. So, play nicely, and he will be just fine, won't he? Easy I say."

Victor enjoyed tormenting people far too much.

"Fellas, if you just leave Miss Jameson in here, someone will be along soon to sort out the clothing situation."

The door closed behind her with an audible click. Thea was instantly on the cuff wrapped snuggly around her arm. She tried yanking it off and sliding it up and down her arm, but nothing worked; it was firmly stuck there.

"Get off, you useless piece of," she stopped herself before she went on an outright rant. "What have I gotten myself into now?" she moaned. "I'm meant to be this all-powerful witch, yet here I am, a prisoner, caught instantly."

The room she was now in was much nicer than the last few she had occupied. There was a beautiful four-poster bed, covered in the finest silken bed throws. The colours ranged from deep red to the softest violet. She ran her hand across one of the fluffy-looking cushions. It reminded her of her pink teddy bear slippers, back when her life was normal.

She suddenly felt home sick. What she would give to see her mother's face, to even know she was okay; to text Jason and for him to reply with one of his stupid dorky one liner's. There was a gentle knock at the door.

"Can I come in, Miss?" came a small voice from the other side.

"Yes," Thea hesitantly replied.

"Master Victor said you were in need of fresh clothes," the

young girl said.

She wasn't any older than Thea; she may have been a little younger, it was hard to tell. She was about Thea's height but younger looking in the face. She had long, perfectly straight black hair that met her waist at its full length, and stunning grey eyes.

"What's your name?" Thea asked

"Chloe, Miss," she shyly replied.

"Hey Chloe, I'm Thea," she smiled at the girl. She handed Thea the clothes.

"I was told to wait for you outside the room," she instructed Thea, then she turned to leave.

"Great, let's look at what I have been given this time," she sighed as she placed the small bundle on the bed. There was a short black dress, a small black shrug and pretty little lace slip-on shoes.

"Not my first choice but not too bad," she thought. She nipped behind the old-fashioned changing screen in the corner of the room and slipped off her blood-stained top and leggings.

Her leg still ached, but not as much as it had before. She had to admit they did a good job on her leg, at least. She tugged the slinky dress over her head and down her body. It was shorter than she would have liked, only just covering her thighs and she slipped her feet into the pretty little shoes; she pulled at her dress once again.

"What do I look like in this?" she wondered. "Mum would hate it for sure," she smiled. "But would Ryder?" the thought intrigued her. "Not the time or the place, Thea," she scolded herself. Moving over to the full-length free-standing mirror, she scrutinised her reflection. Her hair was ruffled and out of place, her skin was pale looking, and deep dark circles had taken up residence beneath her eyes. She had Ryders's blood smeared on her cheek and all across her arms. She liked the dress, though, even if it was a little bit too short.

She took to searching around the drawers of the room. She needed a hair brush. She didn't know why it was so important to impress her captors; she guessed it was just so she could get the chance to be with Ryder again.

"Jackpot," she muttered.

She found a hair brush and a couple of bands in a little drawer beside the bed. She had never been very good at doing her own hair; she was a pony tail only kind of girl. She had mastered a side braid, though and opted for that one. It took a little longer, but she hadn't been told she was on a time limit. Once her hair was neat and she looked presentable, she quickly rushed off to the bathroom that was adjacent to her room. She hastily washed her face, neck and arms. Finding a fresh tube of toothpaste and a new brush waiting for her, she hadn't been so happy to see such simple things in her life.

She finished washing up and sprayed a small amount of the perfume that was sat on the counter. It was a bit strong but better than nothing. One last look in the mirror confirmed that she was as ready as she was ever going to be.

Chloe didn't speak to Thea when she came out; she kept her head down and walked ahead of her.

"How sad this girl's life must be," she thought.

"I'm not sad," Chloe thought back to Thea. "You're just not worth the punishment I would receive if anyone found out I spoke to you."

"How can we hear each other? They put this annoying magic cuff on me last night," she shook her arm.

"No idea, guess it has broken or something. Stay out of my

head. I don't want any trouble," Chloe shut her mind off from Thea from then on.

The walk to where Victor was waiting took longer than she thought. They must have wound around and around the house a good few times.

Thea didn't bother taking in the sights. She had to see if she could reach Ryder; seeing as she spoke with Chloe, it should be doable now.

Reaching out with her mind, she had to feel her way to her boyfriend's battered one. It took some time, but soon she felt the familiar energy. She had to be so careful not to touch anyone else's mind. She didn't want to clue them in that she had at least this power back.

"Ryder, can you hear me?" she thought in the gentlest way.

"Hey there, princess," she felt him smile. "How are you doing this? Have they removed the cuff?"

"No, I just seem to be able to do it now. It could be broken, I guess," she suggested.

"I don't think so, sweetheart, they're tough as nails." He informed her. "I'm guessing you're either more powerful that the cuff, or they're allowing you to do it."

"Let's hope it's my power, huh?" she smiled back. "How are you doing? Please say they haven't touched you again," she was so worried.

"No, they haven't been back in yet," he confirmed. "Where are you?" she sent him an image of what she could see.

"That still amazes me that you can send images as well as thoughts," she was sure she could hear him chuckle.

"I have to meet with your dad and his buddies in a minute," she told him. "He gave me clean clothes as apparently I looked a mess," she sent him mock shocked feelings.

"You always look beautiful to me; you know that," he replied. Thea could feel how much he cared.

"Why are they treating me like this? Why haven't I been thrown in a cell as well?" she pondered

"Sadly, he has probably realised he can use you for his own gain somehow, don't ask me how, as I don't know, but he always uses everyone in a way that benefits himself," he added.

She let the thought sink in.

"Hey, do you want to see what I have to wear?" she asked him nervously, trying to change the subject.

"Of course,"

She thought about how she looked in the mirror just before she left the room and concentrated on that, then sent it his way. She was greeted with the strongest feeling of lust and jealously but topped off with awe.

"You're stunning, Thea. I hate that they get to stare at you, and I don't," she blushed.

"I've got to go for a bit. I just arrived at the door."

Chapter 18

The room was packed with middle-aged to elderly men. When Thea stepped through the door, everyone fell silent.

"Ah, here is our guest at last," Victor proclaimed as he held out his hand for her. She worked so hard not to show her disgust as she reached out her slender hand and grasped his. It was ice cold, just as she imagined it to be.

"Don't you clean up nicely, Miss Jameson," he noted; she just nodded at him polity.

"Be nice, be nice, be nice," she instructed herself.

"Let me introduce Miss Thea Jameson," he called out to the whole room. They all looked at her. She felt very exposed right then. "This is the high council of the Nightshade coven; you have no idea how honoured you are right now," the whole room laughed.

From the back of the room, a tall blond man was pushing his way forward. Thea had a funny feeling before she even saw him. He stopped right next to Victor. Thea had her back to him, to begin with, but the intense feeling grew and gnawed at her.

"Let's get a better look at your special VIP Vic," the man with the silky-smooth voice said.

"Aren, my friend, I was so hoping you would make it, it has been a long time, and I would have hated for you to have missed out on our little gathering today." Victor completely ignored Thea, but she didn't miss a word he said.

That name, Aren, made her blood run cold. Stood right

behind her was her father. She was inches away from learning what he looked like for the very first time.

Victor reached round and grabbed Thea a little too hard by the elbow.

"Thea dear, I would like you to meet my very close friend Aren Ravens."

Thea turned but angled her eyes to the ground; she wasn't ready to meet her father yet, not like this. He stuck out his hand.

"The pleasure is all mine," Aren said politely. Thea looked up and took his hand. His face was a picture. He dropped her hand instantly.

"Ellen?" he breathed, staring at her. Fear, shock, regret, and if she wasn't mistaken, longing was written all over his face.

"Aren, you look as if you have seen a ghost," Victor noted, placing a hand on his friend's shoulder.

He shook himself.

"Not at all, old friend, your guest here reminded me of someone I used to know, that is all, please excuse me. I have to go," and with that, he left.

Thea was numb; she just stood there, unsure how she was supposed to feel. Victor started to waffle on about something or another; she wasn't listening.

"Young Thea here came looking for my treacherous son," Victor told the room. They all chuckled. "Yes, believe it or not, my waste of space heir has managed to get someone to have feelings for him," more laughter followed.

Thea was seething, she hated this man, yet she held her tongue. She could feel her power tingle in her fingers; but she forced it back. She couldn't allow these people to sense it. She wasn't ready to unleash it all yet; she barely knew how to control it as it was. She had no plan on how to save Ryder. She had to be careful.

"This young lady will be able to help us learn more about one of the rival covens, the Brockmoors," he continued. "My son is not very forthcoming, but I'm sure Thea will be, won't you, my dear?" he squeezed her arm.

She stared blankly at him. He finished his little speech, and the room continued to talk amongst themselves.

"What am I doing here?" she spoke through gritted teeth. "Why am I not locked up like Ryder?" she genuinely didn't understand.

"You are the key to forcing information out of my son. If he thinks you are with me, he will start to conform. If I lock you up, he will fight to free you," Victor explained.

"You're a piece of work, you know," she managed to smile while insulting him.

"Ah, ah, ah, little girl, play nice, or you won't get back to your precious little boyfriend," he sniggered. He had her exactly where he wanted her.

"Who was that guy you introduced me to?" she tried to sound genuinely curious.

"Aren?" he asked. "He's a member of the council like me; he just hasn't ascended as of yet."

Thea was going to probe more about her father, but Victor was pulled away; he had received an urgent message from one of his scouts. Thea watched the changes in Victor's expressions very closely.

"I wish I could hear what they were saying," she thought.

"Then make it so, Isamcey," a small voice said inside her mind. Zans was with her once more.

"Master Victor, one of the scouts has sent news that the Brockmoor coven is beside themselves," he reported. "The

204

Willows have been searching for a certain witch for a long time, they finally found her, and the Brockmoors want her back as well as her daughter," he continued. "There was apparently sighting of our kind around those parts lately, and they think we have a hand in the matter. They are out for blood," the messenger said.

"Well, yes, we were there, but only to retrieve my useless excuse for a son," Victor confirmed.

"No sir, Master Aren's men were sighted," the messenger stated.

"Aren's men? Whatever for?" Victor genuinely didn't have a clue why he would be there, but Thea did.

The whole pace of the day had changed as quickly as it had started. Victor was not impressed but still had a room full of very important people and Thea to deal with. She watched him try to maintain his composure; she could tell it wasn't easy. He sent the messenger off to fetch Aren, something was up, and he wasn't happy that he didn't know what it was.

Thea reached out with her mind to call Ryder; she had to tell him what was going on. It wasn't going to be as easy this time, though, not with the sheer number of minds in this room. She had to tread very carefully.

"Ryder, are you there?" she pushed gently at his mind. He took a while to answer her.

"Yes, I'm here. Sorry, I think I passed out," he tried to joke

"Not funny, Ryder. I know you were just asleep," she paused. "I just met my father," she blurted out.

"What? Who's your father?" he questioned her. She was so nervous, more so than she thought she would be.

"Well, I confronted my mum after you told me about your life and how members of your coven ascend," she stalled. "You said about your father's friend never ascending."

Ryder pushed in. "Aren is your father?" he might as well have shouted at her, the way the words slammed into her mind.

"Yes, apparently so." Ryder was silent. "I have to go; your dad is coming," she hastily replied and slammed her mind shut.

"What to do with you," Victor's voice made her cringe. "I have a lot to do, but that doesn't mean I'm finished with you, don't mistake this as letting you off, do you understand?" he sneered at her.

"Yes," she nodded.

"I want answers from you, so you have a choice to make, and if I were you, I would make it well," he said with his hands on his hips. "Your infatuation with my son might just help me after all. I have to go for a while, so you can either go back to the comfort of the guest wing, or you can go back to my son's cell. The choice is yours," he grinned at her. "But if you choose my son, you will be giving me the answers I desire when I ask, without a fight, or he will suffer for it, do you understand?" he laughed; he really was a piece of work.

"Ryder, every time," she didn't even hesitate.

Victor's face twitched up in a vile grin, she knew he would enjoy her choice way too much, but she didn't care. To get back to Ryder and plan a way to escape was all that mattered. She was sick of standing in this room full of equally despicable men all gawking at her. She tugged at her dress, wishing it was longer, she knew they were enjoying her discomfort, and she hated it.

"As you wish, young lady, I personally would have picked the guest wing over a dirty cell, but who am I to say how the mind of a confused little girl works," he laughed. "Take her back to cell three twenty-two, and only bread and water are to be given," he ordered one of his henchmen. "Oh…okay, a blanket as well, then you can't say I'm not a kind person," he sneered at Thea before

206

she was led off by the elbow.

Thea was marched back down the long corridors of Ryder's family's estate, so fast she tripped a couple of times, angering her escort. She would get dragged back up roughly and told to move herself, or she would be sorry.

When they reached the cell door, all was quiet; which was a relief. If screams had been coming from the cell again, Thea didn't think she would be able to cope with it. She wished she had full control of her powers. She was getting better at it, but it still wasn't second nature to her. She wanted to just blast her way out of here, dragging Ryder with her, but she knew that wouldn't achieve anything. She would only start a war, and that was the last thing she wanted.

Right now, all she wanted was Ryder and to be left alone for a while. God knows how long she would have, though, before Victor came for her again.

The door swung open, and a rough, scratchy brown blanket was thrust into her arms.

"In you go, precious, see you soon," her burly escort said and shoved her roughly through the open door; it was slammed quickly once she was in.

The room was dark and smelt awful. She looked around for Ryder; it was so quiet in there. A heap in the corner moved slightly.

"Ryder?" she spoke softly; she didn't want to startle him.

"I'm okay. I just can't move," he told her. "They put a hex on me. I'm stuck here, and I can't move around. It doesn't sound too bad until you can't get up and stretch… it's starting to hurt a bit," she could hear the pain in his voice.

Thea was angry; the hairs on her arms felt prickly. She wasn't about to let him stay like that all night.

"Hold still; I'll sort this," she said quietly. Energy rushed from her fingers and crawled all over Ryder's skin like thousands of tiny ants. Within seconds he was released from the punishing grasp of the hex his father had put on him. He audibly sighed.

"Stay put. I don't understand how I have gained the use of my powers again, but apparently I have. The cuff hasn't been removed at all, so it doesn't make sense," she whispered. "I can feel it is limited. I don't what them knowing I can access it, though," she rushed over to him and muttered into his ear. "I don't know if they are watching us," she said.

"I know, but damn I need to stretch," he moaned.

She couldn't help but chuckle at him.

"I have missed you so much, even your moaning," she chuckled. He tugged her by the arm, making her fall onto him so he could kiss her. It must have hurt him; with all the punishments he had received.

"I missed you too, now stop stalling and tell me about Aren. How the heck is he your father?" he insisted.

Thea knew it was coming, but she still didn't find it easy to talk about it, even with her boyfriend.

"I didn't know what to say when he came over, he thought I was my mum! He even called me Ellen," she told him. "He actually looked pale, and a little bit nervous, plus my mum said she was with a guy called Aren, so if you put two and two together, it's simple really," she told him.

"The weird thing is, Victor had no idea Aren was near Brockmoor; he wasn't happy that your coven was accused of taking my mother," Thea's voice shook. "Dan got hold of my mother Ryder, he most probably handed her over to the willows by now, and I'm stuck here. Aren went looking for me without the rest of the coven knowing, so I don't know what is going to happen now."

Ryder hugged her a little tighter.

"It's okay. Once we get out of here, we will rescue your mum, then work out what to do about your father! I promise you're not in this alone," he reassured her, but she just looked devastated.

"I'm so new to all this. I barely know anything when it comes to magic. I just keep winging it and hoping it turns out right," she blurted out. "To top it off, I have been told I'm the Isamcey, which I have no clue about, just that I can control a lot of power. It would be great if I actually had a clue how to control my power at will and not randomly," she almost forgot to breathe as she rattled everything off.

Ryder was in pure shock.

"You're Isamcey, for real?"

"Well, yeah, the elements told me so," she replied, confused. "Everyone keeps getting really excited by it, but I never asked to have this, to be this all-powerful person. I don't want the responsibility," she sobbed. It was the first time she truly allowed it to sink in. "Oh Ryder, what do I do? It's too much too soon, I can't do this; it would be different if I had grown up knowing about my power, but I didn't," she confided in her boyfriend.

Ryder held her for a while, reassured her, and helped her relax.

"First things first, let's think of a way out of here, then we can face everything else," he said; he knew they were most probably being watched. With all his girlfriend had just said, it was just a matter of time before the door flew open and she was ripped away from him again. Right now, his father didn't truly know what he had in his grasp.

Footsteps echoed from the walls outside the cell. All had been quiet for hours. Ryder had spent ages talking Thea through ways to access her power more quickly and on demand. They had decided that the next time Victor came for Thea, she would channel Ryder so he could help to focus and direct her power. Then she could stun him and whoever was waiting for them. She had more than enough power to do that easily.

The footsteps stopped outside their door; the door opened, but instead of Victor standing there, it was Aren.

"Quickly, come with me before it's too late," he spoke to Thea, who was in shock. "What are you waiting for, girl? Come on," he urged her, ushering her over with his hand.

"Not without Ryder," she told him.

"Blast it, child. Why are you making this so hard?" he growled at her. "If he's found to be missing, all hell will break loose," he told her

"Okay, I'll stay here then. Thanks for dropping by," she mocked him.

Aren was so angry that Thea could see him turn a couple of shades redder.

"Fine, but hurry up. I don't know how long we have," and he walked out of the cell.

They followed Aren closely out of the cell block.

"Why are you helping us?" Thea asked her father.

"I have my reasons. Now be quiet before we get caught," he didn't even turn around.

It was so early no one was up yet. The moon was still visible when they left the building. Aren led them around all the detection spells that were set every night. If they tripped even one, the whole place would be on them in an instant.

"Where are we going?" Ryder asked once they were far

enough away.

"Somewhere we can chat without being disturbed," Aren told him.

Aren was tall, toned and handsome. Thea could see why her mother had liked him, but she couldn't see any resemblance to herself in him. He had light brown hair, bright blue eyes and what looked like blue tattoos across both arms. He wasn't dressed like yesterday when Thea had first seen him. Today he was in a black shirt with the sleeves rolled up to the elbow, dark grey trousers and dark walking boots. Thea refused to speak; she didn't know what to say to this man. Yes, he was her father, but she didn't know him. In fact, all she knew was his name and that he had abandoned her.

By the time she brought herself out of her thoughts, she found they were back in the forest, heading towards an old cabin. She could just see it poking out from behind the trees.

"For the last time, boy, shut up. I don't have to explain anything to you," Aren was getting annoyed with Ryder. Thea hadn't even heard him asking Aren questions.

"I have a right to know, Aren. You are meant to be my godfather, yet you keep something this big from me. Does my father know?" Ryder was persistent.

"Of course he doesn't. No one knows," Aren spat back.

"I am here, you know," Thea grumbled. "You could talk to me instead of about me! You know, seeing as I am the subject and all," she reminded them.

"Would you two just get inside? Then we can talk." Aren shut the door behind them.

The heads of all kinds of animals hung from the rustic wooden walls. The floor was covered in their pelts. The furniture was old, worn and very sparse.

"What is this place?" Thea asked as she looked around.

"My old hunting cabin," he replied as if it was normal for everyone to have a hunting cabin.

"Okay then, anyway, why are you helping us? Weren't you at Brockmoor to take me just like the Willows were?" Thea accused him. She glared at him so fiercely, anyone else would have been afraid, not Aren; he grinned at her.

"You look so much like your mother," he smiled, making Thea angrier than before.

"Oh yeah, the one you left to raise a baby on her own, the one you claimed to have loved until crunch time, then you just walked away," she spat at him. "Whatever it is you want from me, you're not getting it. You don't deserve anything from me. I owe you nothing," she added. He sighed.

"I'm your father, Thea! At least give me a chance to explain," he said

"Why should I?" she folded her arms and stared him down. "I'm seventeen years old. The only reason you want anything to do with me now is because you want to ascend," she said as a matter of fact. "Oh yeah, I know all about that."

Aren looked at her; he looked ashamed.

"That's not true, Thea," he sounded tired.

"Oh please, like I'm going to believe that," she scoffed.

"It was true, yes; when I first found out about you, I panicked and made her leave," he sighed. "I had to live up to my father's name. I had to impress him. Being with someone who wasn't of our coven and of the same or higher status as me would have been catastrophic. I would have lost everything; I would have been disowned," he pleaded. Thea couldn't believe him.

"You don't have a clue, do you?" she questioned as she shook her head.

"What do you mean?" he asked.

"It doesn't matter; it doesn't change anything anyway. Seventeen years is a long time," she added.

"Look, Thea, once I found out Ellen had disappeared, I went looking for her. I couldn't find her, and I have searched for you both ever since. I regret turning you away that night; I'm sorry," he sounded so genuine. He looked to Ryder. "Your father knows I was in the area now; he was never meant to know. He has a lot of questions for me, but I have managed to evade them for now. We both know it won't last, Ryder, don't we!" he stated. "I have kept this mission to myself for a very long time; I didn't want anyone to know that I couldn't have children because I already had one. If anyone found out then, Thea would have been in mortal danger," he continued. "Thea was conceived out of love, but rules were broken, and in our community, that is unforgivable," he finished.

Thea was conflicted; she didn't know what to do or what to think. She reached for Ryder for support; he was right there with her.

"If you really mean what you're saying, then you will help me rescue my mother. I'm sure the Willow coven has her," Thea told him.

She knew she would have a better chance with his help than without. Her head was whirling right now. Everything he said swam through her mind.

"It sounded as if he did truly care and regretted his decision, but that doesn't change the fact he abandoned me," she thought. "Do you think we can trust him?" she asked Ryder in her thoughts.

"Hmm, I don't know, he's my godfather, and I have known him my whole life; I always thought of him as a cool uncle. I want to say yes! but I think we need to be careful, don't tell him about your power or about being Isamcey. Hold as much back as you can," Ryder warned her. "Please try to contain as much of your power as you can; don't let him see how amazing you can be. I don't want him to use you or exploit you for what you are. I worry that this could all be a ploy to get you to trust him, so he can use you to finally ascend. You have to give your blood willingly; it can't be taken by force," he finished.

"I'll do my best, but you know as well as I do that if the elementals want to be heard, they make sure they get heard regardless," she looked worried.

"We can deal with it when it happens," he squeezed her hand. Thea could feel shame roll off Ryder.

"What's wrong?" she probed.

"It must look like I helped my father gain his power willingly," he answered. "I just wanted him to see me, accept me, to be proud of me. So, I gave my blood willingly, in hopes he would change his ways with me... he didn't. All it did was help him become the monster he is today," Ryder admitted.

"None of this is your fault, Ryder; he is accountable for every single one of his actions, not you," she soothed him. Their silent conversation was cut short; Aren spoke up

"We will need to leave right now if we want to get far enough away before they notice you're both missing. Once they see your empty cell, this place will be teaming, and I won't be able to do anything about it," Aren explained.

"Fine, let's go; you have to lead as I have no idea how to get there, oh and please say you have a car as I really don't want to walk," Thea added.

"Yes, I have a car," Aren laughed as he ushered them out the door once more.

Chapter 19

Creeping around the forest in the early morning wasn't Thea's idea of a good time; she was still wearing the stupidly short black dress and flat lace shoes; and she was freezing.

Aren's car was parked a little further away than she had anticipated.

The forest at this time looked and smelt totally different from when she was last creeping around in it. It smelt damp like something was off. Everything mushed under her very unprotected feet, and the rain from last night's downpour had collected on the leaves above, drenching her each time the wind blew.

Aren led the way, with Ryder walking at the back; he was more limping than walking. His father's men had done a good job at bruising every part of his body. Thea trudged along in the middle, shivering.

Twenty minutes passed before the banged-out car came into view. Rust covered a good proportion of it, and weeds were growing out of the doors in places.

"You must be joking," Ryder said once he saw their transport.

"What's wrong with it?" Aren asked. "Yes, it's not like my normal car, but I wouldn't be hiding that one out here now, would I! let's be realistic," he rationalised.

"Will it even run?" Thea worried.

"Of course it will; don't be silly," Aren scoffed as he

rummaged around under the car until he pulled out a key. "Ah, there it is, okay, in you get," he told them.

Ryder yanked open the door, pulling the weeds out in the process; he held it open for Thea to climb in. Aren got in the driver's seat while Ryder slid in next to Thea. True to his word, the car started.

"Ah ha, see, I told you so," he said, sounding a little relieved. Thea allowed a small smile to cross her lips but only for a moment.

"Thea, you're freezing," Ryder sat next to her and rubbed her bare arms and hands.

"Your father's choice of clothing doesn't cater for early morning walks in winter," she shivered.

"Reach under the seat in front of you. I think there might be a blanket under there," Aren called back. Luckily there was.

"So, what's the plan?" Ryder asked. He directed his question at his godfather.

"We will head towards the Willows, I guess," he replied. "Other than that, I don't know; I'm just going to go with it when we get there and hope a plan comes to me," Aren admitted.

"So, we are driving into this blindly. I don't get you Uncle… I mean, Aren. You're one of the Nightshades' best, you always have a plan, and you always win. What's different this time?" he questioned him.

"This time, my daughter and her mother are at stake. That's what's different," he snipped back. "I know right now you don't trust me, either of you, and I can't help that. I can't do anything to prove that to you," he said. "Thea, you don't even know me, so I don't blame you, but you, Ryder; you grew up with me, you know how I am. You at least should trust me, but I understand you love Thea and your loyalty to her is outstanding. I commend that; I just hope, in time, you will both see I'm on your side," he tried to not let his sadness show.

The rest of the car journey was quiet. Ryder would fall asleep quite often; he hadn't regained his strength yet. He had gone through days of punishment and was only given minimal food; he was weak. Thea sat beside him, wrapped in the old musty blanket with his head rested on her shoulder, and his hand clasped in hers. She couldn't describe the relief she felt knowing she had managed to help get him out of the torture he was living through.

All the time they were apart was a living hell for him, one she could never have imagined. She had doubted that she would ever see him again. Finding him the way she did, haunted her whenever she closed her eyes. She may only be seventeen, but the way she felt about him was powerfully strong and not something she ever wished to stop. She would move heaven and earth for him, which she had already proved.

She vowed that once she had rescued her mother, she would go back and show the Nightshades that they had made a grave mistake when it came to Ryder. Victor wouldn't be smirking at her for long.

She sat silently for a while, listening to Ryder's gentle snores. Her father knew not to try and talk to her; the feelings she was giving off weren't very forthcoming. So, he made the right move and just drove. She was lost in thought right then, and she didn't have a place that she could call home. She had hoped that the Brockmoor coven would have turned out okay and possibly have become her new home. But right now, she didn't know who to trust.

The way the Willows had hunted her down at the club instantly wrote them off for her, and she would never become a Nightshade coven member.

She missed Jo, but her bother was unforgiveable. The things he had done to the people she loved was unforgettable, and she wasn't about to give him any satisfaction by turning up there again. Her mind kept driving back to Jo; she really did feel she had a connection with her. She had always been so kind and understanding.

She was just beginning to drift off into a much needed sleep when Aren slammed the breaks on, throwing the two of them right into the back of the front seat.

"Sorry, are you okay?" he called back.

"What the hell, Aren?" Ryder shouted.

"Sorry, mate, I can feel strong magic up ahead, and there is no way I'm taking us through that if they're looking for us, which I wouldn't be surprised about, seeing as all three top covens seem to want my daughter now," he finished.

"Stop calling me that. My name is Thea," she told him groggily.

"There is an old service only rout back up the road; we will go that way," he said. "Not long now, about an hour to go taking that road," he added.

"Where are you taking us exactly?" Thea asked.

"We will be right in the middle of Brockmoor territory and Willow territory. Seeing as we don't know who we are running from any more, being in the middle will be the safest place for now."

The Benford Hotel sign shone out brightly up ahead. A cheap hotel was the destination for the night. As they pulled into the car park that was littered with empty drinks cans and crisp packets, the heavens opened on them once more. Aren parked as close to the door as he could.

Slamming the doors, they ran for the entrance. It was no

good, though; the rain was that super wet kind of rain; you only have to be stood in it for a couple of seconds, and you're drenched.

Aren secured them a room for the night and led the way down the dimly lit corridor. There were two single beds, a small bathroom that needed a clean, a broken lamp and a nasty-looking kettle that none of them intended to use.

"I don't have any more clothes to wear," Thea shivered.

Ryder tried his best to warm her, but it was useless.

"There was a shop not far up the road. I'll go there and see if I can get you something, but please promise me you'll stay here, don't leave or do anything stupid," Aren requested.

"I won't be long," he said his goodbyes and left.

"Hey, come here," Ryder beckoned her over. He had sat down on one of the beds with a towel. "Let's see if we can get you at least a little bit dryer, okay?" he smiled at her.

Thea plonked herself down next to her boyfriend and let him dry her wet hair with another towel wrapped around her shoulders.

"I think there's a dressing gown in the bathroom. Going by the state of this place, it's probably not that clean, but it's dry," he pointed out.

Thea shuffled off to the bathroom. Moments later, she returned wrapped in the once white dressing gown. Ryder pulled the duvet cover off the other bed and pulled Thea onto the bed next to him, and draped it over her.

"The door is locked, and Aren will probably be a little while. I'm right here, so try and get some sleep," he kissed her head. Agreeing, she snuggled down next to him, but she wouldn't let him go.

"I love you, Thea Jameson," he whispered into her ear as she

219

fell asleep.

When she woke up later, Aren was back with bags full of clothes for her and Ryder. He didn't know their sizes, so he bought loads of different things in many sizes, hoping something would fit.

It was early afternoon by the time they had all washed up, changed clothes and had something to eat. Ryder ate enough for three people his size; it was the first proper food he'd had in weeks; he wasn't going to waste it.

Thea nibbled at a current bun Aren had brought back, but she wasn't really interested in it. She was still toying with the idea of whether to contact Jo or not. She hadn't spoken about it yet as she really didn't know if she liked the idea herself.

She sat and watched Ryder finish his third packet of crisps. She took in his face, his hair, the way he sat, everything. Worried she might lose him again, she wanted to enjoy these moments.

"You won't lose me again because I'm not ever leaving," the thought popped into her mind. He looked at her sideways and flashed her a cheeky grin. She loved it, even if he was covered in bruises.

"Hey, how did you know I was thinking that? I have learnt to shield my mind," she mused.

"I guess you're just open to me. We must be linked now," he winked at her. "I like that," he added. She went a deeper shade of red. "That will never get boring. Red is your colour," he teased.

Thea shook her head; she was going to just go with it.

"Right, I have been thinking we need help, and I think we can trust Jo, not her brother Dan though, just her," she told the other two. Ryder thought about it for a moment.

"You're probably right, but her loyalty to her brother might be a problem," he voiced his concerns. "Does she know what you are," he sent the thought to Thea

"I don't know, but she has probably figured it out," was her simple reply. They both looked to Aren.

"Don't look at me. I don't even know this Jo. I'm just here to show you the way and help with the rescuing. If you feel you can trust her, then go for it," he answered.

"Okay, we need to get a message to her," Thea said. Aren looked confused

"How?"

"Believe it or not, I'm quite good at mind-reading, which includes sending and receiving messages," she said smugly. Her father didn't say anything, but she could see he was intrigued. "I'll try now," she said.

She sat crossed-legged in the centre of one of the beds and closed her eyes. She concentrated as hard as she could on Jo. A few minutes passed, and nothing, but just as she was about to give up, she felt Jo's mind. She knew the feel of her presence distinctively. It was Jo who she had practiced mind blocking with.

"Jo, it's Thea. Can you hear me?" she called out. Instantly Jo jumped and replied.

"Thea, bloody hell. Where are you? Are you okay? Who is with you? What happened?" question after question got fired at her so fast it was a bit overwhelming.

"Jo, I'm fine, but I need you to listen; it's very important," Thea started. "I am with Ryder and a friend," she chose not to reveal who Aren was yet. "We need your help. We can't come back to Brockmoor; I don't trust it there. It was Dan who had Ryder sent away. It was Dan I ran from when he took my mother," she told Jo feeling her shock and pain over her brother as Thea revealed what happened.

She tried to send Thea a message, but Thea stopped her and carried on.

"Please, just listen right now. I know it's hard to believe, but please trust me. I need you to," Thea sent the words to her, putting all her emotion behind them.

"Okay, you can trust me, but promise you will explain everything, and I mean everything," Jo demanded.

"I promise, now can you meet us here," she sent Jo an image of the hotel they were staying at.

"Yeah, I'll be there soon," she replied and was gone.

"She's on her way; we better get ready just in case I am wrong about her.

It wasn't long, and Jo pulled up in a little red car and parked alongside Aren's. Thea peered through the shabby old curtains and saw her get out of the car, locking it behind her. She was alone. Thea threw the door open and ran to Jo, hugging her. She was so happy to see a friendly face.

"Thea, it's so good to see you and in one piece too. Are you okay?" she hugged the younger girl back.

"I'm fine, but we need to save my mum. Dan has been on the warpath lately. He handed Ryder straight back to the Nightshade coven and covered it up. Ryder has been tortured for days," Thea told her.

"I can't believe Dan would do such a thing; I'm not saying I don't believe you; I'm just shocked," Jo clarified.

"Yeah, well, he did, and we got word from a Nightshade scout that the Willows have my mum, and they are after me still. We need to go and get her," Thea added. Jo's face fell.

"I think we have a problem," she said.

"What? What is it?" Thea asked her.

"The Willows have taken Simon and Dan; they won't give them up until you are handed to them," Jo told them.

Dread settled in Thea's stomach.

"Is that why you agreed to meet us here? Are you going to hand me over to them to get your brother back?" fear sounded in her voice, her power stirred.

"Thea no, that is not what I intended at all. I was hoping we could work out a way to sort this all out," Jo was saying when the door opened, and Ryder stepped out, followed closely by Aren.

"What is he doing here?" Jo was instantly ready for a fight.

"He's on our side, believe it or not; and he's my father," Thea assured her.

"Your father!" she was so shocked she let her defensive spell go, which was one good thing at least.

"Yes, I am, and if you even think of selling my daughter out, you'll have me to deal with." He stared at her point-blank.

"By the way you reacted, my reputation precedes me," Aren finished. The tension coming from Jo and Aren was almost too much to bear.

"What do we do then?" Jo asked.

"We go and get my mother!"

The end

223